启发精选纽伯瑞大奖少年小说

出事的那一天
On My Honor

[美] 玛丽昂·戴恩·鲍尔 著
邹嘉容 译

河北出版传媒集团
河北教育出版社

图书在版编目(CIP)数据

出事的那一天：汉英对照 /（美）鲍尔著；邹嘉容译.
—石家庄：河北教育出版社，2011.6（2014.9重印）
（启发精选纽伯瑞大奖少年小说）
书名原文：On My Honor
ISBN 978-7-5434-8247-0

I.①出… II.①鲍…②邹… III.①儿童文学－中篇小说－美国－现代－汉、英 IV.①I712.84

中国版本图书馆CIP数据核字（2011）第110627号

冀图登字：03-2011-004

ON MY HONOR by Marion Dane Bauer
Copyright © 1986 by Marion Dane Bauer
Published by arrangement with Clarion Books, an imprint of Houghton Mifflin Harcourt Publishing Company through Bardon-Chinese Media Agency
Simplified Chinese translation copyright © 2011 by Hebei Education Press
ALL RIGHTS RESERVED.
本简体字版 © 2011 由台湾麦克股份有限公司授权出版发行.

书　　名	出事的那一天	
作　　者	玛丽昂·戴恩·鲍尔	
译　　者	邹嘉容	
策　　划	北京启发世纪图书有限责任公司	
	台湾麦克股份有限公司	
责任编辑	袁淑萍　刘书芳　杨兆鑫	
装帧设计	春　龙	
出　　版	河北出版传媒集团	
	河北教育出版社　www.hbep.com	
	（石家庄市联盟路705号，050061）	
发　　行	北京启发世纪图书有限责任公司	
印　　刷	北京天来印务有限公司	
开　　本	880毫米×1230毫米　1/32	
印　　张	6.25	
字　　数	80千字	
版　　次	2011年8月第1版	
印　　次	2014年9月第3次印刷	
书　　号	ISBN 978-7-5434-8247-0	
定　　价	15.80元	

版权所有·翻印必究
如有印装质量问题请与印刷厂调换　电话：010-60695281
发行电话：010-59307688

序

我向文学献辞

梅子涵

世界上有不少的文学家。他们写书给我们看。

他们写诗、写小说、写童话，让我们过上了文学的生活。

那真是一些才华横溢的人，多么能够想象和讲述！

他们编出吃惊的故事。他们说啊说啊总能说出吃惊的感情。

他们成功地写了一个人，无数的人就知道了这个人，这个人就成为世界的人。

他们智慧地表达了一种思想，这个思想就成了灯光，我举过头晃动，你也映照，大家都提在手里照来照去了。

他们写出一个个句子，连成一个个段落，语言、文字就这么变为了完美的一篇、完整一本。在文学里面，我们能读到语言、文字为自己兴奋的表情，它们为自己的妙不可言吃惊！

文学的阅读、文学的生活就这样让我们平常的日子里能有喜悦掠过，能有诗意荡开，能有些渴望，能有很多想不起来的爱……

我们开始讲究情调了，注意斯文，注意轻轻地呼吸。

看见了天空的颜色，看见了风筝。

看见黑夜平淡地接在白天的后面，可是活着是不能马马虎虎的。

看见人是活在人格里的，人格都是有一个方向的，文学里的好人也是我们的友人，因为我们喜欢他们的方向；文学里的坏人也是我们的仇敌，因为我们憎恶他们的方向。

序 02

看见梦幻不是空洞的浪漫,梦幻是可以让生活成为童话的。

文学的阅读,文学的生活,让人不舍得离开。

它们成了一个人日常生活外的另一种生活,因而也成了日常生活里的一种生活。

我们就这样既是在文学的外面,也是在文学的里面;我们想念着文学的里面,也响应着文字的外面;我们说着文学里面的故事给文学外面的人听,文学里面的快乐和感动就成为文学外面的日子的部分。

这样活着,珍贵的生命多了丰富,感觉的位置也不是在低处了。

我们在高处站立。

我们看望得很远。

文学就是这么好的一种东西。

所以文学是必须搁在童年面前的;童年必须经常地在文学中。

这不是一件需要举行启动仪式的事。

它越是最简单地开始,越是能最真实地进行。它越是不隆重地被捧在手里了,它就越是在真的接近隆重。

这么说的时候,我就又想起了那本法国小说里的少年,他十四岁,叫扬内茨,是波兰人。波兰被纳粹德国占领了,他住在父亲为他挖的三米深四米宽的洞里,洞在森林里,他的父亲已经战死。不远处的公路上有德国人的巡逻车和子弹,可是他却从洞里走出来走到另外一个洞里去。那里聚集着二十几个游击队员,很多都是年轻的大学生。他们有的是走了十几公里的危险道路而来,他们挤在这洞里,聆听一种声音,这种声音就是音乐。他们聆听肖邦的钢琴曲,它正从一张唱片里放出来。然后聆听一个人朗读童话,童话的名字叫《山丘小故事》,是英国的吉卜林为孩子们写的。

在这个藏身躲命的洞里,音乐和童话是如此隆重!

年少的孩子,游击队员和年轻的大学生们如此隆重。

因为他们小的时候,这样的聆听和阅读是日常的,所有的盼望都来自记忆。有了体面的习惯的人,甚至会在艰难的呻吟里把隆重安排好。这个十四岁的少年和那些游击队员们,后来解放了祖国。

我把这一些话搁在我们的这一套完美的儿童文学书籍的前面。

这是我对文学的献辞。

我对阅读的献辞。

我对童年的献辞。

我对纽伯瑞的献辞。

这位叫纽伯瑞的英国人,是人类最早的为儿童写书,设计书,出版书的人。他是一个让儿童的阅读快乐着荡漾起来的人。他的生命、他的实业和事业、他的人格名声、他身后的一切,也都在童书和童年的快乐里荡漾。这个杰出的人,在这个非常有重量的儿童文学奖里,一直灿烂了!这么多年来,当那些手里拿着选票的人,把它投给一本书的时候,心里都会珍重地掂量掂量,它会影响灿烂吗?

纽伯瑞奖,盛放进它的奖里的一本本给孩子们的书,于是也就灿烂了。很多年都灿烂。我们把这些灿烂捧到手里吧。

故·事·导·读

填不满的缺口

散文作家　凌拂

出事的时候，乔拼命地跑，只在摔了一跤爬起来的时候，才瞥见自己的脚指头流了血。就好像受伤的是别人的脚指头，荒野的河床长满了蓟花，他完全无视自己脚下踩了些什么。

蓟花是一种生长在河床以及旱地的植物，周身长满了棘刺，而他，赤脚踩过，一点痛的感觉也没有。

生命中的许多过错以及不由掌控的状况，总是发生在预料之外。"意外"为人所不乐见，却又总是有着可循的蛛丝马迹。它非但令人措手不及，更是生命中永远难以填平的缺口，但是，有许多东西要从这个缺口里有新的开始。

一个人的个性及态度，往往决定这个缺口里长出来的是什么；对事情怀有遗憾是非常痛苦的，但是它也教会我们看清自己与面对现实，并且从中学习和调整。

《出事的那一天》叙述的是一个非常令人感叹的故事，压缩在细节中的张力缓慢但是令人惊动，细节的层层转接全在内心，像游丝一样反复。少年的血气、口舌的逞能、激将、意气，所有的事情都像午后闷雷的天空，看似无事，但是压低的气压，惊天动地的风雨，在窒闷无声之中可知又不可知地奔湍而来。

故事中的两名少年，从小一块儿长大，个性却全不相同。

乔是个谨慎有节制的孩子，个性沉稳，但也优柔寡断，常隐藏自己，迁就别人；遇到不喜欢的事，也会勉强自己去做；常口是心非，说些礼貌但不由衷的话；善体人意却不善拿捏真实的自己；一味迁就却未必得到自己乐见的结果。

作为乔的朋友，汤尼显然是个乔未必赞同却也无法违逆的人。汤尼率性，坚持自己，想做什么就做什么，固执地不去考虑别人。对汤尼来说，再无法无天的事也不算什么，他的个性冲动，也自我、莽撞些。他兴风作浪，汩其流，扬其波，善于挑衅，用激将法一次又一次击中乔的弱点，在这个部分，汤尼是完完全全地吃定了乔。除了这些，实在没有什么别的能硬把乔和汤尼拴在一块儿，但是，乔还是交了汤尼这个朋友；因为除了汤尼，其他人好像又都显得有点儿无趣。

事情就是这么矛盾，情绪上一个隐藏自己，缺少决断力；一个粗勇莽撞，带着傻胆，好逞口舌之能。

两个少年在成长的过程中别扭、违拗，既好逞能又好面子，为了逞口舌上的胜利，什么事都有可能在一时之间发生。"我想的"往往不是"我做的"，"我做的"往往和"我想的"不一样，青涩少年，回首时不就错失在那一点抵死的面子上？对于所有成长过来的人，都能了解这点无谓，但是对正值年少的许多乔与汤尼而言，这看起来无谓的事，却正是他们往来交关之处。

这个故事写的是一个朋友的死。两个一起长大的懵懂少年，相处时心里常有一种幽闭的闷气，是一起的友伴，但又不服彼此，言语间充满挑衅；既在一起又相颉抗，来不及找到彼此之间相安的角度，事情就向一个无法掌握的方向流过去了，令人措手不及，一切只为了表示自己没什么不敢。血气之勇是一个永远无法弥补的缺口，但是生命总有一些什么在这里重新开始。

阅读本书，令人心疼这两个只随着情绪走的粗勇少年。作者掌握他们之间无谓的压缩张力，过程描述得很好，让人深刻感受到仿佛是作者的亲身体验。对于乔，有时候我们真是那样，心里想的和嘴里说的不一样，但是碍于同侪友伴的压力，使得我们屈从，不得不违背自己。勉强自己又未必真的快乐没有负担，但在成长的过程中，这是生命中必须经历的学习。

揣测并期待别人替自己选择和做决定，乔一直扮演的就是这样的角色。心里这样想，嘴里却那样说，乔根据自己的判断，一直以为爸爸会替他承担和推托某些事情，谁知从爸爸这个角度看过去，却又正试着想给乔一个新的尝试、新的空间与新的开拓；之所以会误判，是因为生命是个变数，不是常数，而我们却常常误判。

整个故事在情节推叙的表面下，有许多牵动却隐藏的线，出事后乔慌冷的痛楚，本能地使他逃避并寻找借口，但又逃不出内心的承担，这中间有许多隐藏的、无法言说的内心传递，情节推叙过程十分绵密，挣扎的过程令人低回，因为太像真实中的我们自己。懵懂少年的误判与期待，还真令人有一种蒙混的假象与习惯。《出事的那一天》在细节张力上的真实感，令人刻骨，一路读来，是一种很好的思考与映照；只希望这一切都只是过程，那么，未来才能更强壮与完整。

献给马松一家,

他们的生活

丰富了我的童年记忆。

出事的那一天

（中文版）目录

第一章　人格保证……………………001
第二章　变调的承诺…………………010
第三章　滔滔河水……………………017
第四章　漩涡…………………………023
第五章　寻找伙伴……………………028
第六章　求救…………………………033
第七章　一百个理由…………………041
第八章　逃避…………………………047
第九章　焦躁的心情…………………055
第十章　无助…………………………062
第十一章　绝望的事实………………067
第十二章　共同承担…………………072

On My Honor
CONTENTS

Chapter 1	081
Chapter 2	090
Chapter 3	098
Chapter 4	106
Chapter 5	112
Chapter 6	118
Chapter 7	127
Chapter 8	134
Chapter 9	143
Chapter 10	151
Chapter 11	157
Chapter 12	163

第一章　人格保证

"去爬饿死岩？你不是说真的吧！"

饿死岩州立公园①里的那座河谷，岩壁又高又陡，乔一想起来，就忍不住毛骨悚然，更别提去攀爬了。他直盯着汤尼的一对眼珠子说："去年不是才摔死一个人吗？你这么快就忘了？"

汤尼满不在乎地耸耸肩，然后猛地抬起他那辆 BMX 老爷自行车（美国名牌自行车，适于做特技表演）的车轮子，转了一圈。"谁知道那家伙是不是真的在攀岩时摔死的？你敢说他不是直接从岩顶上掉下来的……或是自己跳下来的？"

乔骑着施文（Schwinn）十档变速自行车，他弯下腰来拍了拍挡泥板。根据他的想象，上面应该有很多灰尘

---

① 饿死岩州立公园位于美国伊利诺伊州的中北部，湍急的伊利诺伊河在这一带形成了十八个峡谷，其中一个深达三十八米，就是饿死岩。根据民间传说，曾有一队印第安人在和别族作战时，受困并饿死在这里，因此而得名。——译者注

才对。"反正，如果你要去攀岩，我就不去。我才不干这种蠢事呢！"他故意用十分不以为然的口气说话，心想：也许有那么一次，能说服汤尼放弃满脑子的馊主意。

"贝茨先生，你要是怕的话，那就别爬吧！"汤尼说。

"谁怕了？"乔舔了舔干巴巴的嘴唇，"我只是想去游泳。你没看，今天一定又是个大热天！再不然，我们去盖树屋也行！我爸爸帮我们带了一些木头回来。"

"树屋不急着盖，"汤尼说，"我们可以等回来再弄！游泳就免了，我今天不想下水。"

"你什么时候想过要游泳了！"乔忍不住嘀咕了一句，他觉得市立游泳池那湛蓝的池水，好像在眼前闪闪发光。事实上，汤尼和乔想做的事很少有一致的时候。有的时候，连乔自己都很纳闷，为什么他会喜欢跟汤尼在一起。就算十二年前他们恰好出生在同一条街的面对面的两户人家里，而且生日相差不到一个星期，那也不代表什么啊！一定还有些别的理由！

自从乔满六个月大、妈妈又回去上班的时候开始，汤尼的妈妈——沙宾斯基太太——就一直是乔的保姆。所以，乔跟汤尼可以说是一起流着口水抢玩具长大的。不过，乔现在只有白天的时候得去汤尼的妈妈那里报到一下，让她知道他去哪里就行了，因此，他们实在没有什么理由非要整天腻在一起；只是，除了汤尼，其他人都显得有点无趣。

"拜托啦,乔!"汤尼说,"你今天跟我去公园,我明天就跟你去游泳。"

乔一想到游泳池那道湿湿滑滑、又长又弯的溜滑梯,就不舍地叹了口气。明天,明天万一下雨了怎么办?而且,谁知道到时汤尼又会冒出什么点子……跟今天的一样疯狂。就算没有新鲜的玩意儿,他也一定赖账,装作忘了自己说过要去游泳的话。乔一边想,一边又整理了一遍放在车座后面袋子里的午餐盒。

一个人去游泳实在无趣,可是,总比去公园的岩壁送死要好吧!他记得公园里到处竖立着警告标志,提醒游客不要离开步道,以保安全。这个汤尼却偏偏要去爬河岸的岩壁!

贝茨家的前门开了,乔的爸爸带着四岁的弟弟巴比走出来。巴比的保姆也是沙宾斯基太太。每天早上,乔的妈妈得赶时间上班,所以都由爸爸负责让巴比吃完早餐,再去沙宾斯基家。

乔看到爸爸牢牢地拉着巴比的手,心里突然有了盘算。他决定故意去问爸爸准不准他骑车去饿死岩。当然啦!攀岩的事,他一个字也不会提。反正,他爸爸一定会觉得骑自行车去州立公园,太远又太危险啦!他爸爸一向很在意这一类的事。到时候汤尼一定会很生气,怪他多嘴；可是，"按说"他们是应该问的，不是吗？至少，这么一来，汤尼就不能说他不去是因为胆小了。

"爸爸！早！"乔打着招呼，对自己的盘算十拿九稳。"我可不可以跟汤尼一起骑自行车去饿死岩？"他故意稍微地背对汤尼，以免看到汤尼那张臭脸。

乔的爸爸停下脚步，对着街屋顶上刚升起的太阳眯起了眼睛。"骑自行车去饿死岩？"他重复了一遍乔的问话，好像伊利诺伊州还有别的饿死岩似的。

"对！"乔说，"不算很远啦！大概只有十五千米！"

"正确距离应该是十三千米！"爸爸一边说，一边领着巴比走过来，"不过，还是挺远的！"

"我也要去！"巴比嚷嚷起来，"我也要去公园，好不好嘛，爸爸？好不好嘛，乔？"巴比絮絮叨叨的声音，让乔联想到蚊子那种在空中挥之不去的嗡嗡声。虽然妈妈说，这是每个四岁小孩必经的成长阶段，可是乔觉得一整年都这样也未免太久了一点。

"今天很热，"爸爸不理会巴比的哀求，继续说，"而且那条公路很窄……不但斜坡多，还弯来绕去的。"

"让我去嘛，爸爸！"巴比的声音越来越大，也越来越尖，"让我跟乔一起去，好不好？"

"不行！"爸爸摇摇头，"我还不确定要不要让他们两个去呢！好了，你别吵，现在就过马路到沙宾斯基太太家。小心哦！巴比，要小心车子！"

尽管这条街一向安全，几乎没什么车子往来，他们的爸爸还是习惯要叮嘱两句。巴比嘟着嘴，心不甘情不愿地走开了。

"我们会小心的，爸爸！"乔可以听见自己的声音也像在哀求，而且完全不输给巴比，一副他真的很想去的样子。

"真的！贝茨先生，我们一定会很小心的。"汤尼也加入了恳求的阵容，"其实，公园没那么远……而且今天不是假日，路上没什么车的！"

乔的爸爸用手指头使劲地挠着头发，挠得它们一根根都竖了起来。"我知道车不多，可是这条路一会儿上坡，一会儿子下坡……骑起来可一点儿都不近。"

"我们要是累了，就马上回头。"汤尼说。

乔没再说什么。对他而言，说服了爸爸才真的是输了！不过，他相信，爸爸是说什么也不会同意的。

乔的爸爸皱着眉头，仔细地检查了一下他俩的自行车。乔原以为爸爸看到汤尼缠在车把上的绳子会起疑。"那是攀岩的时候用来把我们绑在一起的。"汤尼早对他这样宣布过了。不料，爸爸对绳子视若无睹，只问了句："你们连午餐都准备好了？"

"没错！"汤尼用手拍了拍和绳子一起系在车把上

的午餐盒。

乔的爸爸又转过来问乔说:"你知道你下午还得送报纸吧?"

乔点点头。他当然知道。或许,这也可以拿来当借口。

"要是你们没有力气骑回来,怎么办?汤尼的妈妈没有车,我可不希望到时候得请假去接你们。"

汤尼看着乔,示意要他再加把劲说服自己的爸爸。

"我们不会把自己累到没有力气的。"乔只好不情愿地开口。

爸爸的眼睛闪了闪,好像有所觉察。谁知道,他只是转向汤尼,追问了一句:"你妈妈知道吗?"

"知道!"汤尼轻松地回答。乔不必看他的脸,就知道他在说谎。

汤尼是那种大大小小的事情,只要能不说,就绝不会跟妈妈说的人。至于他妈妈,因为要忙着照顾其他的小宝宝,也很少主动问他。

乔的爸爸竟然点点头,就这样信了汤尼的话——大人们有时候实在是蠢得令人受不了。还好,他随即又赎罪似的提出另一个建议:"你们怎么不去另外一边呢?你们可以去通往郊外的乡间小路兜兜风呀!那里的路很平坦,很好骑。"

"可是，那边哪里也到不了！"汤尼马上抗议，"而且景色也单调，除了马路两边的玉米地，什么也没有。"

最重要的是，没有岩壁可以爬！乔偷偷地在心里插了句话。

乔的爸爸叹了口气，刚扣上夹克的扣子，一会儿又全解了开来。那神情让乔的胃抽痛了一下。他该不会真的在考虑要不要答应吧？要是换成汤尼的爸爸，一定想都别想，早就斩钉截铁地说"不行"了。

"乔，你自己觉得呢？"爸爸问，"你真的有力气骑到公园再骑回来吗？"

乔可以感觉到汤尼灼热的眼光紧盯着他，看他怎么回答。

"嗯！"虽然喉咙好像被什么东西卡住了，他还是硬挤出来几个字，"没问题！"

乔的爸爸摇了摇头："我不太相信！不过，话说回来，让你们两个小家伙儿今天晚上累一点儿，也不是什么坏事。"

乔的两条腿差点软了下来。他爸爸居然答应让他们去了。

"这样，我们就可以好好地锻炼一下腿上的肌肉喽！"汤尼得意扬扬地夸起口来。

乔的爸爸仍然注视着乔，"你能不能以你的人格保证?"他说,"你们一定会留意车子,除了公园以外,不会去别的地方!还有,你们一路上都会很小心!"

"我以人格保证!"乔一边宣誓,一边严肃地在胸口划了十字,还把右手也举起来。只不过,他在心里又多附了几句话给自己听:除了去饿死岩送死以外,我什么都不会做,到时候你可别后悔!

他爸爸又盯着他看了好一会儿,才点点头说:"好吧!我想你已经够大了,可以跑到远一点的地方玩了。"

"来吧,伙计!"汤尼兴奋地大喊大叫,还伸出一只脏兮兮的手掌要跟乔对拍。他随口又加了句:"我有骑施文的优先权哦!"

乔拍了拍汤尼伸过来的手掌,并顺势拧了拧他的脸。汤尼的一双眼睛又黑又亮,眼神里满是笑闹,他还嬉皮笑脸地露出一截牙齿,看起来真像马戏团里的小丑。乔只能在心里摇头叹息。

"想得美,我才不会先让你骑我的自行车。"乔说。但他心里清楚得很,对汤尼来说,他答不答应其实都一样。

乔的爸爸仍然没有把目光移走,乔只好又顺势说了句:"谢了,爸爸!"他努力让自己听起来像是发自内心的高兴,还用两片僵硬的嘴唇勉强挤出一个微笑:"真是太谢谢你了!"

爸爸又点了点头,脸上的表情仍然很严肃。"要记得,儿子!"他最后一次强调,"你是用你的人格保证的!"

"好!"乔嘴里这么说,心里却想,爸爸为什么不提醒他们离那些岩壁远一点,"我知道。"

第二章 变调的承诺

乔眼睁睁地看着爸爸开车离去,觉得自己好像被背叛,被陷害了。这样一来,他要怎么去跟汤尼解释:他刚才只是随便问问而已;还有,从一开始,他就没想要跟他一起去攀岩?

"让我骑你的自行车,好不好?乔!"汤尼拜托着,"好不好啊?"

乔叹了口气。看汤尼雀跃的神情,别人还以为他们要去过圣诞节呢!哪像是要去玩命!"好吧!但只限去的时候!"他知道回程的时候——如果还能活着回来的话,一定会很庆幸有十档变速,可以省点力气。

汤尼的BMX是传了三个哥哥之后才转到他手上的老爷车;挡泥板不见了,把套没了,连原来的红漆也褪得只剩下一些斑点。不过,它倒很适合做一些旋转和下溜的特技动作。乔的那辆银色十档变速自行车可以骑得飞快,也可以骑得很慢，就是别想变出什么花样来。

乔伸长了手臂去扶汤尼的自行车，同时把自己的车交给汤尼。"好了！"他说，"我们出发吧！"

他们不到十分钟就骑出了小镇。经过学校的时候，汤尼对着他们上年度上课的那间六年级的教室，吐了吐舌头。乔为了发泄自己的心情，也依样照做；其实他一点也不讨厌上学。

热得好像在嘶嘶作响的艳阳，高挂在蓝得像从油漆罐里泼洒出来的天空。小镇被他们抛在身后，越来越远。公路两旁长满了高高的青草，他们就从这些高高低低的青草丛中穿过去，沿途还不时听见野云雀的叫声从沟渠那边传来。

汤尼旺盛的活力沿路展现无遗，他一会儿骑成"8"字形，一会儿转圈圈，把整条渺无人迹的公路完全霸占了。他还曾经试着骑直角转弯，差点把乔的施文自行车给摔坏。

乔则是一个劲儿地向前骑。到了威米兰河谷的大陡坡时，他身子向前倾，两只脚拼命地蹬，蹬得汤尼的老爷自行车哼哼啊啊地求饶。威米兰河谷只是他们路经的第一个河谷而已。他知道待会儿上坡一定很费力，不过，这倒让他又燃起了一线希望：说不定，汤尼还没骑到公园就没有力气了。

不一会儿,轮子就转得让人来不及踩踏板了,乔只好让车子自己滑行;自行车的速度越飙越快。他想瞄一瞄汤尼追上来了没有,结果头稍微一偏,自行车的前轮就晃个不停,他只好目不转睛地直视前方,让车轮稳定下来。两个轮胎在平滑的柏油路上嗡嗡地叫,呼呼的强风迎面而来,就像有人在后面拼命地扯他的头发,硬逼着他撑破眼皮似的,使他的一双眼睛又干又痛。

快抵达桥边——也就是两面山坡之间的最低点——时,车速简直像在飞。他估计以这样的冲力,至少可以冲上对面斜坡的一半,而不需要再踩踏板。

经过桥上时,速度快得连看一眼桥下的河都不可能。不过,乔不用看也知道下面的景观是什么样:一摊红色的烂泥水,上面还泛着些看起来油油腻腻的漩涡。等到自行车的速度渐渐慢下来,他的两条腿可以跟得上轮子的节奏时,他就开始一边踩踏板,一边估量自己还得趴多久。快没力气踩了,他就挺起身子,利用自己的重量把踏板强压下去。

最后,连两腿也实在软得使不上劲儿了,乔只好下来推车。汤尼骑的是十档变速的施文,这会儿总该追上来了!

"这坡可真陡啊!"乔朝身后丢了句话,却不见汤尼回应,他回过头去寻找汤尼。

原来汤尼还在刚刚那座桥上。他将自行车随意停靠在桥上粗大的铁栏杆上，身子则伸到栏杆外窥探下面的河流。

"嘿！你这无赖！"乔左右察看了一下有没有来车——就算生爸爸的气，他还是会保持这个好习惯——然后调转车头，又溜下刚爬上来的斜坡。他知道待会儿要再从坡底骑上去，可就没那么简单了。可是，汤尼才不管这档子事；也许他应该跟汤尼要回自己的自行车。

"你在看什么？"乔拉抬起前轮，用后轮溜到汤尼的旁边。

"看河啊！"汤尼一边回答，一边又把身子伸得更外面一点，"我在看这条老人河。"

"你在说什么？老人河是密西西比河的分支，这里是威米兰河！"

汤尼没有答话。乔知道对汤尼来说，这种纠正毫无意义。只要汤尼想把威米兰河叫成老人河，别人也拿他没辙。他在学校的时候，就是那副德性……即使考试也一样，都快把老师气疯了。

汤尼挂在栏杆上的样子，就像杂技演员在表演荡秋千。乔不敢再看下去，只好别过头，衷心地祈祷汤尼小心一点。

不知道为什么，他忽然像小时候那样很希望汤尼是他的兄弟。他俩可以当双胞胎——那种不需要长得像或者性格很像的双胞胎。反正,沙宾斯基家有那么多小孩,少一个汤尼也没多大关系。就算他们开出以人换人的条件,他可一点也不介意把爱号叫的巴比送过去。

"你知道了吧!"乔说,"要上那个坡可没那么简单。"

汤尼直起身子嘻嘻笑,他那身晒得红彤彤的皮肤把一口白牙衬得更亮了。"我在想,我们可以不必去饿死岩。"他说,"我有一个更棒的点子!"

"比去饿死岩更棒的点子?"乔很好奇,也很高兴终于可以不必为了攀岩跟汤尼吵架。

汤尼在栏杆上跳起舞来,好像要用他的脚说话。"没错!反正我们有的是时间,可以爱做什么就做什么。"

"对啊!"乔马上热切地附和。

"我们甚至可以去游泳。"

乔简直不敢相信自己的运气有这么好。"好啊!"他兴奋地大叫,还伸出手掌要跟汤尼对拍。

可是汤尼不但装作没看见,还弯下腰,用手指着从桥下蜿蜒而过的那摊棕红色的河水。"今天很适合去游泳。"他说。

乔瞪大了眼睛。"在这条河里?"他不敢相信地又问了一次,"你想到这条河里游泳?"

汤尼故意耸耸肩："不然你以为是哪里？"

"在这里？那还不如到你家厕所游泳。"

"谁敢这么说！"

"我爸爸说的啊！谁说的！"

"我爸爸说的啊！"汤尼故意模仿乔的语气，把声音说得又高又尖，还带点娘娘腔。

乔决定对汤尼的嘲弄置之不理，也决定不提他们出发前对爸爸所做的承诺。"你知道威米兰河是禁止游泳的，谁也不能下水。这种河很危险……有很多深不见底的洞和暗流。有的时候还有漩涡呢！何况，河水脏得要命！"

"搞不好还有鳄鱼呢！"汤尼突然换上了正经八百的语气，可是一双眼睛仍然在飞舞，"这些水之所以这么红，搞不好就是那些被鳄鱼咬死的人流的血染红的。"

"威米兰河才没有鳄鱼呢！你以为我连这个都不知道？"虽然明知汤尼只是在逗他，乔还是不自觉得涨红了脸，"这是河水流经红色的土层造成的，你听懂了没有？红色的土层！"

"那就对了！"汤尼说着，交叉双臂抓住衣衫，把上衣从头顶脱了下来，"如果没有鳄鱼，也没有人流血，我就要下去游泳喽！"

他就这么丢下乔那辆自行车，呼啸着冲下桥，闯进路旁的矮树丛里,还把他那件淡蓝色的上衣当做套马索似的拿在头顶甩来甩去。

"快来吧,乔!"他回头大喊,"谁跑得慢,谁就是三脚猫!"

第三章　滔滔河水

乔看着汤尼挥着两只手，一路呼啸地跑下陡峭的斜坡，冲到河边。他不禁摇了摇头。刚才汤尼穿过的那些油油亮亮的绿色植物，很可能是有毒的常春藤呢！

乔瞥了一眼自己那辆施文自行车，汤尼显然没想过要把它藏进路旁的草丛里。乔先将汤尼的老爷车靠着栏杆停下，再推着自己的施文下桥，轻轻地平放在桥下的草丛中。他本来想学汤尼，把那辆老爷车随便搁置在桥上；不过他终究没这么做，因为如果汤尼的车被偷，只怕永远都不会再有第二辆了。

在威米兰河里游泳！没见过比这更疯狂的点子了，简直比去攀岩还可怕！乔一面摇头，一面把汤尼的老爷车也推过来放在他的车旁。这才走到河边。

"你有没有听到我的话？"乔走向站在岸边的汤尼，"这水脏得要命！更可怕的是里面还混杂着一些你看不见的化学物质和废水。"

汤尼对他的话置之不理,兀自脱掉身上的牛仔裤和内衣。在乔还没过来之前,他早就扔掉上衣,踢掉球鞋了。"至少,它是湿的吧!对不对?"他故意这么问。

"我说过了,"乔回嘴说着,"这里跟你家的厕所没什么两样。"

汤尼才踏进水里,肮脏的河水立刻吞噬了他的双脚,一点痕迹也不留。他回头看乔,又笑嘻嘻地说:"我家厕所的水不够多!我以前试过一次。"

"我相信!"乔回答。他想让自己的语气听起来具有杀伤力;哪知道汤尼回应给他的,却是威力更强大的笑脸。

"你要不要下水?"汤尼回头喊。这个时候,水已经没过了他的膝盖。

"我要等着看你溺水,"乔回答,"我得等着,到时候才能通知你的家人。"

"让我爸妈别担心!"汤尼丢过来一句话。

"让你妈别等你吃晚餐!"乔又回嘴。

说着,两个人哈哈大笑起来。笑声渐停之后,汤尼说:"喂!你到底是要下水,还是要像傻瓜一样站在岸边看?"

"谁要像傻瓜一样了!"乔说着用左脚搓掉了右脚的球鞋。

水温正好,沁凉得让人起鸡皮疙瘩,却又不至于很凉。

一波波的水流经过他的腿边，就像是在为他按摩一样，令他顿觉神清气爽。他从来不知道这里的水流如此强劲。从桥上往下看，河面一片平静，几乎看不出流动呢！

"要小心水流！"他站在几尺开外，靠近上游的方向，对汤尼叫道。

"哎呀！"汤尼用双手掐住自己的喉咙大叫起来，"水流！我被水流卷走了！它把我吸进去，把我吞掉了！"他哀号着向后倒了下去，整个头消失在被激起的水花泡泡下面。

乔站在原地静候。过了一会儿，汤尼突然又站起来，而且变成了一只从沼泽中破水而出的史前怪兽。河水从他的脸上汩汩地流下，他两手低垂，身体弓着，脖子伸得长长的，头还向前突出。

"够了吧！"乔说，"如果要游泳的话，我们就去游泳池！在那里游可比这里好多了。"

汤尼直起身子说："为什么？这边很好玩啊！"

"可是游泳池有溜滑梯……还有别的小孩！"

"谁要溜滑梯……还有别的小孩？"汤尼回答，"而且，我这不就是在游泳吗？"说完，他又把自己脸朝下地投入水中，四周依然溅起不小的水花。

"看起来他好像连怎么游泳都不太会！"乔忍不住自言自语了起来，但他很快就推翻了这种想法。因为对一个好朋友来说，这种假设有点不够义气。虽然汤尼不喜欢游泳，但偶尔也会跟他一起去游泳池玩。不管大家做什么,汤尼都会跟着做;只不过他们大部分时间都花在从滑梯上溜到浅水池里,或者互相舀水泼来泼去。

乔渐渐放松心情,把自己浸到更深的水里,还换成狗刨游了几下。不过,他可不想为了让泳姿好看一点,就把脸放进水里。对他来说,游泳池的人工蓝水和氯的气味还可以忍受;而这条河的味道就像死鱼一样,让他想吐。

"也许我们应该每天来这边练习游泳。这样,说不定我们明年就可以加入中学的游泳校队。"汤尼这么说。

乔停下游泳的动作,站了起来。"如果每天都来这里,一定会被逮到的。"

"被谁逮到?"汤尼问。

"我哪知道!反正,就是一定会被逮的。说不定是哪个开车经过桥上的人!"乔抬头望了望上面的桥,连一辆车子的鬼影子也没见到。

汤尼摇摇头:"贝茨老兄,你知道吗?有时候,你说话的样子真像你老爸。"

乔感觉到一股热潮涌上了他的脸:"那又怎样?"

"在树上要小心哦!儿子!"汤尼模仿着乔的爸爸,"别伤着!巴比,过马路的时候要看一看,那些车子根本不长眼睛……"

汤尼在模仿的时候,乔一直向他逼近,到了他身边,伸手用力地推了他一把。不过汤尼早有防备,不但没退半步,还反过来也推了乔一把。

乔晃了晃手臂,让自己平衡下来。他发现肚子里憋了一早上的怒气,这会儿就要爆炸了。这个死汤尼有什么资格取笑爸爸?"至少,我爸爸不会用皮带抽小孩。"他脱口而出,并握紧了拳头,靠近汤尼。

汤尼的脸色霎时一片铁青。乔马上就后悔了,觉得自己不该拿汤尼的爸爸来嘲讽。其实,他并不知道沙宾斯基先生是否真的用皮带打过汤尼。他只见过沙宾斯基先生边抽裤腰上的皮带,边追着汤尼跑。他当时觉得那个场面挺滑稽的……当然,也很吓人!

汤尼往乔的头部挥了一拳,乔轻易地闪过了。汤尼比他高,比他壮;幸好,反应比他迟钝。

他们站在那里狠狠地彼此互瞪了好一会儿。两个人都气喘如牛,拳头高举。忽然,汤尼转身朝岸边涉水而去。

"你要去哪?"乔问。

"去饿死岩!"一句冷冷的回答丢了过来,"我要去攀岩……自己去!"

乔的一颗心开始往下沉。他既不想一个人骑自行车回镇上,也不希望汤尼独自去攀岩。"噢!拜托,汤尼!"他恳求着,"我们待在这里就好了。这里也挺好玩的啊!"

"跟在你家的厕所游泳一样好玩吗?"汤尼头也不

回地说。

乔想都没想地脱口而出:"厕所也很好啊!"而且为了取信于汤尼,他还把自己整个人从脸到脚给丢进水里,并游了几下到汤尼的前面才站起来。

可是,汤尼还是怒气未消地讽刺了一句:"你这么说,是因为你不敢去攀岩。"

这句话立刻重启了两人之间的战火。"你说谁不敢?"乔质问汤尼,"不敢的人是你!你知不知道!我敢打赌,你连……"他迟疑了一下,看看四周有什么东西可以拿来跟汤尼单挑,有什么是他自己笃定不怕的,"连游到那边的沙洲都不敢!"他手指着约四十米外,露出河面的那一块小小的、黑黑的沙洲。

汤尼眯起眼睛,朝着乔所指的方向凝视。"那有什么好怕的?"他轻蔑地说,"我敢说这整条河都不会比这里深。"河水环绕在汤尼腰际,形成了一个尖锐的"V"字形。

"才怪!河里多的是比这里深的地方。"乔说,"因为河床本身高高低低的,很危险,所以才会禁止游泳。"

"就算有三米深,我也不怕!"

乔靠了过来:"你的意思是说,你接受我的单挑喽?"

汤尼抬起了下巴:"当然!除非你连游泳也不敢。"

"看谁不敢!"乔说。

第四章　漩　涡

乔起先用蛙泳游了出去，游了没两下，换成了狗刨，又游了没两下，终于决定把脸放进水里，只有这样才能好好地游。不过，他还是紧紧地闭着眼，每游几下就抬起头来，瞥一瞥沙洲，调整一下方向。湍急的水流一直推着他往下游去，只要稍不留意，就会错过沙洲。

乔可以听到汤尼在他后面狂乱地跟水作战。一会儿吹气，一会儿吐水，两只手噼噼啪啪地猛拍个不停。他真不知道自己以前怎么没有发现汤尼游得这么糟。

乔用脚尖踩了一下河床，喘口气，然后瞧瞧背后的河岸。他使劲地抹了抹脸上那些不敢想象有多脏的水。汤尼在他的后面紧急地停下。乔反身对他说："你要是不游得好一点，明年休想加入游泳队。"

汤尼的胸口喘得好像已经游了好几千米。"所以我才说要每天都来练习呀！你跟我一起，我就会进步，我们两个都会进步。"

"那去游泳池练习不就得了?"乔说道,他自觉一向比汤尼成熟明理,"那边比较干净,也安全多了。"

"那干脆去大街上练习算了!"汤尼接腔,"让所有的人都看得到我们。"他仍然上气不接下气的样子。

"别人看到了又有什么关系?"

"关系可大了!你想让朗德,还有施密特他们发现我们在做什么吗?要是被他们看到了,他们一定也会吵着要来练习,好加入游泳队。"

"那……就让他们练习啊!有什么关系?"乔觉得很纳闷,这一点也不像平常的汤尼。汤尼一向是大家的朋友,他受欢迎的程度,连乔都常常吃醋,不希望有这么多人跟他一起分享和汤尼的友谊。

也许,汤尼知道自己游得很糟,怕丢面子吧!他说不定从来都没有像其他小孩一样,去青年会的游泳教室游过,可是他偏偏又是那种打死都不愿意承认自己有什么不会的人。

有一回,汤尼宣称自己是高空弹跳高手。他把床单往自己的手腕和脚踝上一绑,然后就从他家楼上的窗户跳了出去。事后汤尼说,他之所以没有成功,是因为跳下来的地方还不够高;医生则说汤尼命大,从那么高的地方摔下来,竟然只摔断了一只手臂。

"来呀！"汤尼用挑衅的语气说，"是你说要游到沙洲那里的，你现在就要认输了吗？"

"你确定你游得到吗？"乔盯着他朋友气喘吁吁的胸口说，"我觉得你看起来好像很吃力。"

汤尼推了他一把，差点把他推倒。"给我游！"汤尼下令。于是，乔再次投进水中。汤尼跟他同时出发，可是没划两下就落到了后头。乔可以听到他在后边又吹气又喷水，像条鲸鱼。

应该没那么糟吧！乔对自己说。他这会儿已经找到了适合自己的节奏，也发现了足以对抗水流、让自己前进的划水角度。也许汤尼是对的！在这条河里游泳是一种很好的训练……既然爸爸认为他已经够大了，可以有多一点的自由，来这里练习也未尝不可。

乔又改成了侧泳的姿势，这样比较能修正自己前进的方向，也比较清楚还得游多远。他看不到游在后面的汤尼，反正，也不需要看，只要用耳朵听，就知道汤尼在哪里了；汤尼简直像部老旧的发动机，一直发出噪音。

只剩十米了。乔又用脚尖轻触了一下河床，再向前看。沙洲旁的水流不断地冒着泡泡、漩涡，看起来水势比别的地方湍急。他低下头，继续用自由式游，并不断调整方向来对抗往下游的滚滚水流。

每一次转头换气，他都大口大口地吸气。与其说是累，不如说是有点紧张。在河里游泳可不比在游泳池。游泳池的池边近在咫尺,要是累了,随时都可以上岸。不过,话说回来,即使是在河里,他也游得蛮好的。说不定,到秋天的时候,他就真的有资格参加校游泳队了。

他早该想到来河里练习的,这个主意其实并不赖。汤尼这家伙的最大优点就是满脑子有数不完的点子。等他俩都游到沙洲的时候,他可得好好地道个歉,承认自己不应该说汤尼爸爸的坏话,不应该讽刺汤尼不敢游泳。

"成功了!"他高喊着,他的手一碰到沙洲的泥土,人马上站了起来,"我赢了!"

没有人搭腔。乔回过身来察看。

在他背后,只有绵延的河水,平滑、闪亮、又红又黄的河水里,并没有汤尼的踪影。事实上,好像没有一丁点儿的线索可以证明乔刚才不是自己一个人游过来的,不是一开始就只有自己一个人来河里游泳的;但他清楚地知道,他的确是和同伴来的。

他气急败坏地推着河水往回走,好像要推开阻挡他的千军万马。"汤尼!"他高喊着,"你在哪里?"

除了他自己又尖又细的声音,像遥远的猫叫一般,从岩壁那边弹回来外,再没有其他的回音。他继续推开河水围成的墙,向前走。

或许,汤尼早就回头了。或许,他正躲在岸边树丛的某个地方，等着看乔焦急的模样。

"够了！汤尼·沙宾斯基，我知道你在玩什么把戏。赶快出来！不管你在哪里。"

没有人回答！树丛那边连一丝窃笑或是衣服的窸窣声都没有。

"你这猪八戒，汤尼，你要是敢动我的衣服……"可是他明明看见他那一堆衣服还好端端地摊在岸边，尤其是那件红色的上衣。

"汤尼！"他开始歇斯底里地向前冲，嘴巴猛喘着气，好像快窒息一样。汤尼一定是躲起来了，一定是上了岸，躲在某个地方……偷笑。没别的可能了！

他的脑袋一片空白，弄不懂到底发生了什么事，直到他一脚踩空，深深地陷进水里，才发现脚底下的河床忽然不见了！那种感觉，就好像踩到了太空中的黑洞似的。当他又呛又喘、挣扎着游出水面时，才终于什么都明白了。

原来汤尼不会游泳——至少不是真的会——而且，他溺水了！

第五章　寻找伙伴

乔立泳了一会儿,恨不得看穿河水那虚伪的平静外表。可是,什么都没有!河面上根本看不出丝毫的改变,也没有任何危险的迹象。到底那个洞有多深、多宽?汤尼是在哪里掉下去的?他还在沉没的地方,还是已经被水流带走了呢?一个人能够在水里存活多久呢?

一个接一个的问题像连珠炮似的射进乔的脑袋里,他根本来不及解答。

事实上,他也没有时间去寻找答案。

他猛地潜入水中,像是要用双手把自己的身体给推进河里。浑浊不堪的河水让他张开的双眼刺痛无比。在几近盲目的黑暗中,他一边游,一边到处摸,看能不能摸到一条腿、一条胳膊、一些头发或是什么都好!但是,他只在河床上摸到了一个又黏又滑、好像已经腐烂掉的东西,吓得他赶紧浮出水面。

过了一会儿，他再度潜入水中，四处搜寻，直到河水在他耳朵里面呜咽起来，才又冲出水面，大口地喘气。

汤尼可能已经被水流带到下游去了。乔顺着河水漂到稍远的地方，再试着找一遍。

还是没有！

他第四次潜入水中的时候，被水流带得离岸更远。突然，他发现自己被困住了，一股强劲的水流吸着他、旋转着他在满是淤泥的河床上不停地打转。他死命地挣扎，伸出了手，好像想攀住水流把自己给拉起来。就在这时候，他碰到了一个硬硬的东西。

会是汤尼正好漂到他上头吗？他猛踢着水想游向这个物体，水流却横阻在前。正当他跟着漩涡打转，又快被拖到河床的时候，一个黝黑的，好像是男孩形体的东西，漂到了他的上方，脸向下，朝着烂泥般的河水。

是汤尼！死……死了！而他，乔，也快要死了！他再也没办法呼吸了！他整个肺剧痛无比，胸腔里的空气爆炸般地往外冲，水又一直往下灌。在他上面漂浮的那个东西擦撞了一下他的手臂和腰。原来，这个又粗又硬的东西，不是人体，只是一根木头。乔赶紧攀住了它。当他好不容易把头伸出亮得刺眼的水面时，身体的其他部分几乎都瘫痪了。

他就这样瘫了好几分钟，又咳嗽，又吐水的，一点力气也使不出来,只是任由河水把他从急促的漩涡带到了水流比较平缓的岸边。他的脚一碰到河床,立刻站了起来。

天空,像是一个被翻转过来的瓷碗,盖在他的头上。一只孤零零的鸟在附近的树上鸣叫。

闭嘴!乔想对那只鸟大叫,你给我闭嘴!可是他终究没这么做。他什么话也没说,只是弯下身子来,吐出一些水。说也奇怪,从他嘴里吐出来的河水居然看起来挺干净的。

他眼前的每一样东西都清晰得几近恐怖:吐出来的河水、一棵倒栽在水中的树和树上裸露的根,还有那湍急的河水流向……流向什么地方?是流向伊利诺伊河,然后再注入密西西比河,对吗?

他们在学校上过有关河流的课,不过,他记不清楚了。

他朝四下看了看。平静的水面仍然纹丝不动。河岸上,也没有鬼鬼祟祟的人影……没有人躲藏。说他是全世界唯一还活着的人类,他也不怀疑。

如果让他找到汤尼,如果让他在岸边的某个角落找到汤尼,他说什么也要把汤尼痛扁一顿,一直打到他喷血为止。他一定永远都不要再跟汤尼说话,永远都不要再跟他一起玩了。因为这是一个很龌龊的玩笑,是汤尼开过的最龌龊的玩笑。

霎时间,一阵寒意攫住了他,尽管太阳依然又热又亮地挂在天空。他呆若木鸡地走向摊着衣服的地方。他要穿上衣服，然后……

他愣愣地站在那堆衣服旁边。汤尼的衣服还七零八落地散落一地。

照这情形看来，汤尼绝不可能已经上岸了。因为，就算是汤尼，也不可能光着身子到处跑……只为了开这么个玩笑！乔又转身面对河水。从粼粼河水反射回来的阳光，让他不得不眯起了眼睛。

不可能！不可能！这一切的一切，一定是梦，是一个随时都会醒来的噩梦。

一辆汽车隆隆地从他头上的桥驶过。

"等等！"乔扯着喉咙大叫，整个人终于从刚才的恍惚中回过神来，"停车！帮帮忙！"他猛挥着手臂跑向桥，可是车子已经开远了，没有人听得见、看得见他。他眼睁睁地看着车子驶过桥头，开上另外一边的斜坡。

他呆呆地站着发抖，牙齿咔嗒咔嗒地乱响，过了半晌，才跑回衣服堆旁，顾不得落在地上的内裤和上衣，只一把抓起牛仔裤，急着把两只脚给套进去。他的一双手抖得连裤子都抓不牢，厚重的牛仔布料粗糙地摩擦着湿湿的皮肤；好不容易穿上了裤子，他开始把脚往球鞋里塞，折腾了半天，还是决定放弃；就这么赤着脚，提着牛仔裤，跑向公路；他心想一定很快会再有车经过的！一定会有的!

他拼命地跑,完全无视自己脚下踩到些什么。只有一次,他摔了一跤又爬起来的时候,头低了一下,才瞥见自己的大脚指头流血了;不过,就好像受伤的是别人的脚指头,他一点痛的感觉也没有。即使踩到了长满刺儿的蓟花,他也照样埋头往前冲。他的肺一直用力地呼吸,仿佛空气也像先前的河水一样在阻挡他。

到了公路旁,他又弯下腰来吐了一会儿,才站起来。他必须求救。如果他得到援助,或许汤尼还有救。可是,他从河畔爬上了两边斜坡的公路……上面空荡荡的……什么也没有!连一辆汽车或卡车的影子都没有!唯一会动的,是一只在天空盘旋的乌鸦。

乔茫然地朝着回家的方向跑,背后的河流好像一只潜伏着的怪兽,随时准备出来偷袭!是一只专门吞噬男孩的怪兽!他忍不住越跑越快,一颗心怦怦地捶着肋骨,一双光脚丫噼里啪啦地踩在黑漆漆的柏油路面上。

第六章　求　救

乔爬坡爬到一半,前面终于出现一辆车朝他开来。这是一辆大型的旧船形汽车,有蓝色的车身和银色的挡泥板,引擎盖上还漆着橘红交错的火焰。乔往马路中间一站,死命地挥舞双手。蓝色车子来了个紧急转弯,闪向对面的车道。乔又跟着抢到前面,好像下定决心,绝不让它跑掉。车子只好一边尖叫,一边猛然刹住,距离乔挥出去的手臂不过几厘米而已。

"找死啊!你这家伙!"车里的人对乔咆哮。看他的模样,应该是个十八九岁的青年,留着一头浓密的黑发,两条光溜溜的胳膊肌肉结实。

"拜……托!"乔气喘吁吁的,一句话也说不出来。他弯下身子靠在汽车的引擎盖上,一边调整呼吸,一边想把话从喉咙里面挤出来。"拜……托!"他又说了一遍。

"这个小孩好像病了。"一个金发女孩说。她就坐在那个大男孩的旁边,两个人挨得很近,好像刚才一起驾驶那辆车似的。她一边说话,还一边把身子向前倾,想透过挡风玻璃窥探乔。

"在……河里。"他手指着方向,努力地说,"拜托你啦!"

"什么东西在河里?"男孩问道,显然开始关心起来,"你到底要说什么?"

乔摇摇头,说不出话来。他的脸好像麻痹了。

"你是不是要说有人溺水,还是什么?"男孩抓着方向盘,向前靠过来。

乔默默地点点头。

"快上车!"开车的大男孩下令,并伸手到后面,帮乔拉开车门。

乔颠颠仆仆地上了车,滑进后座,把门拉上。那个金发女孩马上回过头来盯着他看。她的嘴里还吧嗒吧嗒地嚼着一团紫色的口香糖,脸上一副受惊的表情。

车子又在轮胎的尖叫声中开动,然后迅速地下了坡,在桥边的碎石路上停了下来。

"你刚才说是什么人?"男孩询问,他已经下了车,并帮乔拉开车门,"是你的朋友吗?"

"对!"乔说,他爬下车子的时候,终于恢复了一点声音,"他叫汤尼!"

"他从哪边下水的？"

"我指给你看。"乔说。他一走向河岸，刺眼的阳光立刻映入眼帘。那个大男孩跟着乔跑，那个女孩又跟在大男孩后面。她的两只手在胸前晃来晃去的，好像两只大飞蛾。

乔重回河边，一看见河水的景象，一闻到那令人窒息的、死鱼般的气味，双膝不禁软了下来。那个大男孩赶紧扶住他的手臂。

"就是这里？"他让乔站稳后问道。

"那里有一个地方，水突然变得很深……就在那边。"乔指着他认为汤尼沉没的地方。

大男孩一边脱下上衣，一边问："他怎么会在那边溺水呢？"

"我们那时候正要游到沙洲，等我回头看的时候……他已经不见了。我试过找他。我真的试过。"乔说得好像快喘不过气了。看他胸口起伏的样子，很像是在啜泣，实际上他并没有哭。他的眼睛又干又涩，纵使身体仍然在发抖，体内却好像冰封般僵硬。

大男孩甩掉了鞋子和牛仔裤。他踏进河里，犹豫了一下，瞥了瞥烂泥般的河水。

"这些是他的衣服？"女孩问。她把汤尼的蓝上衣抱在怀里走过来，好像这样就能拯救汤尼。

"对!"乔回答。他克制住想叫她别动汤尼的衣服的冲动。

大男孩跳进水里。他先是稍稍地掠过水面,接着弓起身子,再潜得更深一点。

"你要小心!"女孩对着男孩消失的地方喊。

乔跟女孩并肩站着等候。他一度也考虑要下水再找一找,可是一想到那股攫住他、把他往下拉的水流,那个可怕的记忆顿时把他的双腿变得像铅块一样沉重,让他无法再向前挪一步。无论如何,他相信那个大男孩会找到汤尼的。一定会的!

大男孩第一次浮出水面的时候,乔忍不住激动地大叫:"汤尼!"可是,大男孩的手上空无一物。乔只得发出更绝望的叫喊。

"水流可能把他带到那边去了。"乔喊着,手指着桥那边。大男孩点了点头,又潜入水中,这一回他游得更远了一些,一直往下方游了十几米才浮出水面。

大男孩在水里努力地朝各个方向搜寻。他一次又一次地潜水,直到胸口起伏得越来越剧烈,每次要站起来的时候,也变得有些蹒跚。他的女朋友在岸上踱来踱去,口里仍然嚼着口香糖。"要小心!小心!"她不时地说。但是,与其说是对着她的朋友说,倒不如说是对着周围的空气说。

"你在那边找不到什么的,"她看大男孩一度要游到河中央了,心急地大喊起来,"他不会漂到那么远的。"

"如果他真的漂到那边,怎么办?"乔问。但是女孩没有回答,她看起来简直快哭出来了。

乔站在岸边高喊着各个方向指点大男孩去找。到了最后,尽管乔仍然一再地怂恿"再远一点点!"大男孩还是开始往岸边游了回来。他低垂着头,以防河水顺着发丝流进眼睛。

"你不会是要放弃了吧!你要放弃了吗?"乔问道,虽然沉痛的心里早知道对方已经放弃了。

"没错!"大男孩用力喘着气,拾起了上衣来擦拭脸庞,"我要放弃了。"

"可是你不可以!"乔凄厉地哭号着,"你不可以!"

大男孩耸耸肩,一边发抖,一边气喘吁吁地挤出断断续续的话来。

"听着……你……知不知道……一个人……能撑多久……在水里……不被溺死?"

乔没有回答。他不愿意想这一点。他根本不想知道。

"差不多五分钟,我猜。"大男孩弯下腰,把手放在膝盖上休息。"只有该死的五分钟。"他又吸了更深的一口气,"说不定还更短!"

乔掉头就走,沿着河岸走了好几米。那个大男孩的声音仍然追了过来。

这时候,他的呼吸比较顺畅了,开始一口气吐出一大堆的话来:"而且,在我下水之前,你已经耗了多久的时间了?十分钟,还是十五分钟呢?"

乔无话可答。

"而且,你知不知道……"大男孩渐渐挺起了身子,继续说,"要在这样一条河里找东西有多难……这水流几秒钟就可以把一个人带走。也许下个星期就会传来消息,说某个尸体被冲上岸了……但是,也有可能要等到下个月。"

"我们要找的不是尸体。"乔龇牙咧嘴地转过头来说,"是汤尼!是汤尼!"

大男孩用他的上衣擦了擦胸前和手臂上的水珠,摇摇头说:"对不起!小朋友。"

乔全身紧绷了起来。这家伙在说什么?对不起?他有什么好对不起的?他连汤尼是谁都不知道呢!

"笨小孩!"大男孩用力把牛仔裤拉上腰部,嘴里数落着,"你们一开始就不应该到这条河来游泳的,应该要有一点常识。难道没有人告诉过你们,在河里游泳有多危险吗?"他把脚塞进了鞋里,并拧了拧湿透的上衣。"听着!"他说,"你最好快点穿上衣服,跟我来!"

这下子,换成乔喘不过气了。"要去哪里?"他问。

"去警察局！"男孩的声音粗哑，口气很不客气，好像在怪罪乔让这个意外发生，"有人溺水的时候，就必须去警察局报案。"

"有人溺水的时候"，这些字眼像一声声尖叫，在乔的脑袋里回响着。可是，他只木然地跟着说了声"警察局！"然后就瞪着自己的脚看。警察会问什么？他们会问乔跟汤尼到河边做什么，会问乔到底做了什么事，才会连朋友都给弄丢了。

也许，在上警察局之前……他应该先打个电话到爸爸工作的地方。他爸爸一向比较善于解释事情。他爸爸会……会怎么样？"你是用你的人格保证的，乔。"那是他爸爸说过的话。"你们一路上都会很小心！除了公园以外，不会去别的地方！"而现在，乔已经证明了他的人格不值什么，他根本不值得信赖。

"来吧！小朋友。"大男孩说。他的声音虽然还是粗哑，却不凶狠了。他什么都明白吧！他很清楚警察会问些什么样的问题，乔的爸爸又会说什么吧！乔看得出来连这个大男孩也为他感到悲哀。

"不了！"乔猛抬头，穿上上衣，"你们走你们的吧！我的自行车在这里。我自己会去警察局报案的。实在没道理把你们也牵扯进来。你们走吧！"

"他说得对！"女孩抬起下巴说话，一副很懂事的样子；尽管她脸上还挂着泪水。"是没道理！而且，如果我们回镇上的话，我岂不是自找麻烦。我今天打电话请了病假，记得吗？为了要跟你出来……"她伸长手指头，点一点男孩的胸口。

"可是，这一定得报案。"大男孩顽固地说，"而且，必须有人通知小孩的家人。"

起初，乔以为大男孩说的是自己的父母，后来才领悟到对方指的是沙宾斯基家。到目前为止，乔都还没有想到汤尼的父母。现在，他想象自己去按沙宾斯基家的门铃，然后看见沙宾斯基太太，带着满脸倦容和一双悲伤的眼睛来开门。但是门一开，却忽然变成了沙宾斯基先生站在那里，手里还拿着一条粗皮带。想到这里，乔吓出了一身冷汗。就算警察不找他麻烦，汤尼的爸爸也一定会找他算账的。

"我会去报案的。"他说，"我一定会去的。"

第七章　一百个理由

乔把身子紧靠着自行车，一边用力地推，一边跑上坡。他的心跳声像打鼓一般在耳朵里咚咚地响。那个大男孩跟他的女朋友仍然坐在车子里，大概还在争论到底要不要去报警吧！他们的存在，让乔觉得好像芒刺在背，心里很不舒坦。

过了一会儿，他们终于发动车子，隆隆地驶过桥，开上另一边的斜坡，乔立刻停下推车的动作，整个人瘫在车把上喘气。又过了几分钟，他再往后看，车子已经不见了，只剩下一股热气还在空荡荡的马路上徘徊不去。

他慢慢地推着自行车上坡，走到距离坡顶只剩下一小段距离的时候，前面又出现了一辆红色的小汽车。乔连忙挺起胸膛，摆出一副看起来很无辜的表情。可是，等到车子真的开近他身边时，他还是把脸转开了。他想，要是车子里的人看见他的脸，哪怕只一眼，就能看穿他的心虚。

乔的妈妈早说过,他大概是全世界最不会掩饰罪行的人。小时候,每次他在口袋里面藏了块饼干走过她身边,她只需看一眼他的脸,就会问:"乔,你在口袋里藏了什么?"

现在,大概每一个人都可以只看他一眼,就指着问:"乔,你为什么要去河里游泳?乔,你对你最好的朋友做了什么?"

警方又会问些什么问题呢?就算不问,他们又会怎么猜测呢?

乔想着想着,逐渐停下了脚步,一颗心七上八下地猛跳。他不能回去!他就是不能!

他把车头转过来,朝着下坡,背对镇上,背对着通往警察局、沙宾斯基家,还有他父母的方向。他上了自行车,用全身的重量踩住一边的踏板滑出去,把车子的后轮弄得摇来摆去的。这一次,他不要再下来推了。他要加速到足以一口气冲上河谷对面的斜坡。

是他爸爸准许他骑车到饿死岩州立公园的。他就要照办!

一股热辣辣的疼痛在乔的大腿根蔓延开来。他一圈又一圈地踩着踏板,对两旁的景物视若无睹,只在脑海里闪过一幕幕的画面。公园里的森林十分浓密,要想把他的自行车……还有他自己给藏起来，并不难。说不定，他甚至可以在这些岩壁当中找到一个洞穴躲起来。他可以靠着采野草莓和树根维持生活，就像从前那些印第安人一样。传说中，那些印第安人为了躲避敌人而藏身在饿死岩上。可是，他恐怕不能学他们了。因为现在的饿死岩上到处都是步道、篱笆……还有游客。无论如何，当初那些印第安人被敌人困在岩壁上，最后饿死了。这个公园的名称就是这么来的。

一辆卡车轰隆隆地驶过来，巨大的轮子转动时产生的吸力，一直拖着乔和他的自行车靠过去。他只需要放手，就可以把一切都交给卡车去解决。

乔滑向路旁，从自行车上狼狈地摔下来。他到底在想什么？他真的认为自己可以躲起来吗？就算他真的找到了一个地方躲起来，他又能躲多久？躲到他长大……还是死了为止？可是，这一切并不是他的错。是他的错吗？他没有遵守对爸爸的承诺，并不代表汤尼的意外就可以归咎于他啊！

第一个该怪的，就是爸爸！是他允许他们骑自行车去公园的。乔自己根本不想去。

再一个就是汤尼。疯狂的汤尼明明不太会游泳，还坚持要去河里游，简直是疯子。

乔长长地吁了口气。不知怎么的，他觉得心里舒坦了点。他看了看左右,然后推着车子过马路,朝着原路骑回去。他要回家!那才是他应该去的地方……不管发生了什么事。

他把自行车调到最高档,他要用最少的力气,踩出最远的距离。回家!窄窄的轮胎在柏油路上咿咿呀呀地哼了起来!回家!

不过,他得先想好。他得先想好到底要怎么跟爸爸妈妈说——跟沙宾斯基家说——当他们问起汤尼的时候。

他可以跟他们说……跟他们说……说他和汤尼本来骑着自行车要去饿死岩,可是过桥的时候,汤尼停了下来。那时候,天气那么热……而河水看起来……那么清凉。所以,汤尼想去游泳。

这的确是事实,不是吗?

然后,他可以跟他们说他如何试着说服汤尼别去河边,可是汤尼不听他的劝告。汤尼本来就是那种一旦决定要做一件事,任你说破嘴皮也没用的人。可是,这样子一定会让爸爸想起他今天早上做过的承诺。如果爸爸真提起这件事,他就说,他跟汤尼讲过不要去河边。

他可以说自己本来打算一个人骑车去饿死岩,可是天气那么热,又少了个汤尼,要骑那么远,并不怎么好玩,所以,就调头回家了!

这一连串的解释在乔的心里面排列过来,组合过去,直到一切都显得既符合逻辑又完美。为什么他之前没有想到呢？为什么他要逃跑呢？他慢慢地将紧握着车把的手指头一根根地松开，朝着回家的路前进。

当他再度来到那俯瞰威米兰河谷的斜坡顶端时，他停了下来，凝视着马路、凝视着这座桥、凝视着那几乎遮蔽了河水的一排排树墙。他想，要是有别的路可以回家该多好。可以，他不知道有别的路。而且，他大腿的疼痛已经蔓延到了小腿，连肩膀也跟着绞痛起来。就算有别的路，也不一定轻松。

乔握紧车闸，开始溜下陡滑的斜坡，准备过桥。自行车的刹车皮轻磨着轮子发出吱吱叫的声音。

汤尼自己留下来游泳了。这就是乔要告诉大家的。但是，如果汤尼下去游泳的时候，他真的骑车去饿死岩了，至少在折返的时候，他应该会先停下来查看一下……因为，他不会知道汤尼发生了什么事。

乔骑到桥上了。他紧握着自行车的把手，一边慢慢地踩踏板，一边小心地看路。过了桥头，他犹豫了一下，然后跳下车来，把自行车推到堤下，靠着桥墩放。他只是要去查看一下而已……这样，他在向别人解释的时候，人家就不会一看他的脸，就知道他根本没有去查看。

汤尼的老爷自行车好端端地藏在高高的草丛里。

乔慢慢地走向河岸，尽力不去胡思乱想。这整件事，的确很有可能是像他所捏造的那样发生的。他想好的那一套说辞是说得通的。

一只松鼠在附近的树上又叫又喊,湍急的河水也窃笑着流过。汤尼的衣服,除了那件被金发女孩动过的上衣外,都还凌乱地散落在地上。一只袜子高挂在灌木梢,另一只则落在一丛紫罗兰里。

乔想到汤尼的任性,不由得悲从中来。他帮汤尼把散落的衣服收拾好,仔细地叠过,再整整齐齐地放成一堆。那件淡蓝色的上衣,他留在最后叠;叠好以后,还仔细地端详了一下。

不对!汤尼这辈子从来没叠过衣服;除非,他妈妈站在一旁逼他。乔又蹲下来,把衣服弄乱。

他再站起来的时候,河面上的波光攫住了他的视线。河水看起来一如当初那么的无辜。

刹那间,乔无法呼吸了。他的喉咙紧闭着,把一口气堵在胸口,让他疼痛、惊骇得举起了双手,好像要祈求上苍的赦免。当这口气好不容易冲出来时,他也跟着发出了呻吟。

他站在岸边,紧紧地抱住自己摇摇晃晃的身子。

汤尼死了……他死了!

第八章　逃　避

"乔！乔！"砰的一声门响后，紧接着传来怒气冲冲的叫喊声，"乔，你到底在哪里？"

乔躺在床的正中央，呆呆地望着渐渐填上黑影的灯具。他记得刚躺下的时候，灯具的影子还只不过是一个斑点而已，这会儿，它不但横跨了整个天花板，还弯下了墙来，就像是一只不断膨胀的灰蜘蛛。

"乔，你在楼上？"爸爸的声音再次响起。乔无力地摇摇头。

不，他不在楼上！他不在任何地方！难道沙宾斯基太太不是这样跟他爸爸说的吗？电话已经响了一整个下午，再来是门铃声，叮咚！叮咚！叩——叩——嘎啦——嘎啦！一会儿巴比在叫（他显然是被沙宾斯基太太差遣过来的），一会儿又换成沙宾斯基太太在叫："乔！汤尼！"

但是，房子的钥匙在乔的口袋里，没人进得来……除非等到他爸爸妈妈下班回家，才会有别的钥匙。乔就这样躺了一整个长长的下午，等待着爸爸或妈妈先回到家来。在他的预料中，妈妈应该先回来，因为她通常比爸爸早上班，也早一点回家。

大约在两个小时以前，今天要送的报纸就已经摆在门口了。他听到报纸砰的一声砸到了地板，却一点下床的力气也没有。等爸爸妈妈回来的时候，我就可以去送报了。他虽然这么想，却仍旧躺着一动也没动。

"乔！"一声听起来像放炮的大喊之后，门立刻开了，乔的身体也跟着不由自主地跳下床。他脑袋里的血液瞬间往上窜，整个人顿时头晕眼花，几乎站不住了。

"原来你真的在这儿。沙宾斯基太太就说你应该在这儿。"

乔不吭声，只是呆呆地看着爸爸脚下地板上的一个斑点。

"你在做什么？为什么把自己锁在屋子里面一整天？你哪里不对劲了？"

乔的目光落在爸爸的皮带扣环上。

爸爸则巡视了房间一圈。

"汤尼呢？"爸爸问，"沙宾斯基太太说你们一整个下午都躲在这里。"

"汤尼不在这里。"乔说。

"那他在哪儿？"

乔稍稍地耸了耸肩。

爸爸生气地用手使劲地挠着头发。"到底是怎么回事，乔？这不像你……怎么会一个人溜进屋子里躲着，却让汤尼的妈妈在那边担心。"他说着，向乔走近一步，但是乔并没有退缩。

他盯着爸爸的脸庞，等待着接下来一定会爆发……不能不爆发的脾气。爸爸从来没打过他，但是这一回，爸爸不能不打了。"我大概睡着了。"他说，"我什么也没听到。"他用花了一整个下午才凝聚起来的冷静说话。"而且，这里是我家，我想回来就可以回来。"

现在，就是现在，爸爸要打他了！

乔的爸爸垂下了扯头发的手。"这里当然是你的家。"他平静地说，"可是这不代表你就可以把自己关在里面。你明知道沙宾斯基太太白天的时候是要照看你的。要不是巴比看见你闪进门，她还不知道你在这里呢！"

"鸡婆！"乔说。

"什么？"爸爸问，看起来又生气了。

"没什么啦！"

"好。那汤尼人呢？他妈妈想知道他在哪里。"

在河里，乔想，不过，他大声地说："去饿死岩了！"

爸爸歪了歪头，看起来不太相信。"一个人去的？"他问。

"我自己先回来了。"乔说，"饿死岩太远了，所以我先回来了。"这是他原先拟好的说辞吗？他不太确定。

巴比出现在门口。他把两个小拳头叉在腰上，摆出妈妈发脾气时惯用的姿势。"妈妈和爸爸不在家的时候，你们不应该自己待在这儿的。"巴比用他最擅长的"你完蛋了！"的语气说话。

"那又怎样？"乔毫不迟疑地回击。巴比马上泄了气，低下头来，把大拇指塞进嘴巴里。

爸爸审视着乔的脸。"你是告诉我，"他说，"汤尼自己一个人骑车去饿死岩了？"

"我想是的。"乔说。

"他对我说谎，你知道吗？他说他妈妈准他去。可是，我刚才跟沙宾斯基太太谈过，才发现他说谎。"

乔感觉到爸爸的两道目光像烈焰一般地逼过来。他屏住呼吸，心想一切就要被揭发了……可是，他爸爸摇了摇头，转开了双眼："我觉得自己有责任……"

你是有责任，乔想说。不过，他没这么做，他只是淡淡地问道："你要我去找他吗？"

"当然不。"他爸爸叹了口气，"骑自行车来回太远了。而且，你该去送报了。"他转身走出房间的时候，又朝背后大声地说了一句："我要打电话到沙宾斯基家，跟他们说汤尼可能会晚一点回来。"

会很晚，很晚回来！乔想着，心中突然涌起一股很诡异的、想要大笑的冲动。汤尼死了！你难道不知道吗？他想咆啸。可是他爸爸显然不知道，什么也不知道。他猛踢了一下床脚，喃喃自语地说："该死的报纸！"

巴比的眼睛瞪得又圆又大，他爸爸想必也听到了，却没有回头，看起来完全不打算做什么——不管发生了什么事。

"今天我可以跟你一起去送报吗，乔？"巴比问。巴比总是想跟他一起去送报，想跟他一起执行童子军的任务，想跟他一起做他做的每一件事。有的时候，巴比甚至还帮他洗碗盘。真是个笨小孩！

乔通常都不会让巴比去。汤尼倒常常跟着去，因为他有自己的自行车。对乔来说，要载报纸又要载巴比，可不是什么好玩的事。

何况，汤尼真的会帮忙。他不是那种只会问东问西、碍手碍脚的跟屁虫。

汤尼！沙宾斯基家找得到他吗？那个大男孩说尸体可能会在下个星期……或下个月被冲上岸。或许吧！可是，为什么他刚才没有按照自己原先想好的说辞，跟爸爸说汤尼到河里游泳了呢？为什么他不说他自己骑车到饿死岩,而汤尼去了河边呢?那样的话,爸爸就可以告诉沙宾斯基家,然后他们就知道要去哪里找汤尼了呀!不知道怎么回事,他就是没有一句话说对。

"让我去好吗?乔,拜托!"巴比一再地恳求。乔低下头来看看弟弟,看到那张仰起的小脸上满是殷切的神色。他的喉咙突然又紧缩了起来,赶紧把头别过去。

"好吧!"他哑着声音说,"今天你跟我一起去送报。"

"哦——耶!"巴比欢呼起来,拍着那双又短又胖的小手,一跳一跳地出了房门,下楼去。

乔挺起胸膛,深深地吸了一口气。然后忽然停下来,又吸了一口气,再嗅一嗅。空气中弥漫着一股什么味道?简直像……简直像死鱼的味道。乔闻了闻自己的手臂,还有上衣。这死鱼味的来源……就是他自己。

乔把上衣的领口拉到鼻子上,用力一闻。没错!是河水的臭味跟着他回家了……而他爸爸竟然没有发现。

乔赶紧脱掉上衣,从抽屉中取出另外一件穿上。刚穿上的衣服,气味是清新的,闻起来还有妈妈使用的那种柔顺剂的味道——可是,这淡淡的香味根本遮掩不了贴在他皮肤上的那股河水的臭味。

乔走下楼梯,心想,也许没有人知道河水的气味是什么样的吧!

巴比正在门口帮妈妈开纱门。妈妈看起来一脸倦容。她放下了手里的购物袋,走到楼梯口,两只手叉着腰,跟早先巴比模仿她的神态一模一样。"你们今天到底是怎么回事,乔?沙宾斯基太太说你跟汤尼在屋子里躲了一整个下午。"

乔闭上了眼睛,心想一切又要再来一遍了。这就是有两个家长的烦恼,连训话都不能只听一遍。他调整一下自己的呼吸,让脸上的表情舒缓下来,再继续下楼。对于身上的味道,他是无能为力了。"汤尼没有来这里,"他说,"而且,我不是躲,我是躺在床上。"

"躺在床上?"妈妈走过来摸摸他的额头,"怎么了?生病了是不是?"

"没有!"乔让妈妈伸过来的一只冰凉的手贴着头,"只是有一点不舒服!"

"你跟汤尼今天做了什么?"妈妈一边问,一边又伸出了另一只手环抱在他的头后方,好像一定要用两只手,才摸得出他的体温似的。最后,她将目光停在了他的脸上。

"我们只骑骑自行车而已。"浓重的河水味让他的眼睛刺痛起来。她一定闻得到的。她不可能没发现的。

"骑了多久?"

乔倏地低下头去,挣脱了妈妈的手。他朝走廊后退了几步,背对着她。"不远!汤尼打算骑到饿死岩——是爸爸说我们可以去的——可是,我不太舒服,我刚才告诉过你的,所以我就先回家了。"

他不知道妈妈的反应如何,因为,她在他的背后,他又不愿转身去看。

"饿死岩,"她重复了一遍他的话,"那不是很远吗?"

"是爸爸同意我们去的。"乔说,然后,又强调了一次,"是他说我可以去的。"

"嗯!"她轻叹了一下,"你最好快点去送报,免得订户打电话来催了。报纸到得太晚,订户会不高兴的。"

乔觉得全身都要瘫了。妈妈竟然没有闻出河水的味道。她甚至连他在说谎都没有猜到。他松了一口气,却又有种莫名的愤怒。难道这里没有一个人能细心一点吗?

他推开纱门,让它在背后砰的一声……重重地关上。

第九章　焦躁的心情

巴比蹲在门口,努力地想扯开捆住报纸的绳子。他小小、脏脏的手指头抓着打结的地方,一点一点地往上拉。

"别扯了,小笨蛋!"乔掏出口袋里的小刀,"要这样弄!"他割断了报纸上和旁边那堆夹页上的绳子,动作显得很不耐烦。

巴比看着他,嘟起了嘴巴:"你知道妈妈不'意愿'给我小刀。"

"是不'愿意'!"乔粗鲁地纠正,眼睛避开了巴比的脸,"妈妈不'愿意'给你小刀。"

"好啦!"巴比一边说,一边抓起一张广告传单,塞进一份报纸里,结果两样都弄得皱巴巴的。

"小心一点!"乔大声怒斥,并用刀柄敲了一下巴比的头顶,"你这样子,会把全部的东西都弄得乱七八糟。"

巴比的脸马上皱成了一团,哭了出来。"好痛!"他揉揉自己的头。

"当然会痛！多得是让你痛的事！"乔自言自语了一番，但心里的愤怒旋即被羞愧取代了。何必拿巴比出气？这个可怜的小家伙只是想要帮忙而已。乔开始将传单拆开，一张一张地塞进报纸里，再把报纸卷好；这样子，待会儿要送报的时候，比较顺手。多得是让人痛苦的事！他一再地对自己说，除非死了！死了，才能一了百了。

这个想法让他有些不寒而栗。

"你怎么了，乔？"巴比问，"你为什么那个样子？"他忘了自己的疼痛，瞪着一双大大的蓝眼睛。

"没事！"乔说，简单的两个字却像是从齿缝中硬挤出来的，"你要是想帮忙，就快点把报纸装到袋子里。"

巴比接到命令，开始装报纸，一双眼睛仍然不时打量着乔的脸。

"看你自己就好！"乔对巴比大吼，整个人好像又披上一件愤怒的斗篷，"我们没时间了！"

巴比立刻点点头，用最快的速度把乔卷好的报纸一一装进袋子里。

乔虽然手上忙着塞传单、卷报纸，心头的怒潮却难以平息。不过，他终于知道自己愤恨的是谁了。这全都是汤尼的错！全都是！汤尼明知道自己游得有多烂，还执意要到河里游；他自己应该知道危险的！可是，现在汤尼走了，留下他一个人来面对所有的问题。而他，到底要怎么说才好呢？

等他送完报纸回来，汤尼的父母大概早就准备好一堆的问题要问他了。汤尼还没回家，乔。他会在哪里？你是最后一个看到他……还活着……的人。

"该死的一切！随便吧！"乔大叫，并随手把还没整理完的报纸推下门口的台阶，"我讨厌死送报纸了。"

巴比一屁股坐在脚跟上，眼睛大得像要把脸给吞下去了。他先瞧一眼台阶下面，再抬头瞄了瞄乔。"你砸烂了妈妈紫色的花，三朵。"

乔也看了看。那些报纸刚才正散落在妈妈的牵牛花上。

"你要我帮你把报纸拿回来吗？"巴比问，"我想，如果擦一擦，应该还好。"

"好吧！"乔同意了，"你去拿回来。"

巴比下了台阶又上来。他一边捧着报纸，一边偷觑着乔的神情。"还好啦，乔！"他小心地把报纸放下，好像当它们是珠宝一样。

乔摇摇头，想赶走盘踞在他脑海的一团红雾。要是他现在可以逮到汤尼，他一定会……一定会……可是这太荒谬了！他会做什么？又有谁能做什么？打汤尼一顿？

想到这儿，他哽咽地大笑了；说是笑，却更像啜泣。

巴比看得目瞪口呆，一张脸绷得紧紧的。他用小小的白牙紧咬着下唇。"你还好吗，乔？"他问。

"很好！"乔说，"我没怎样。"他重新开始整理报纸，"我还活着，不是吗？"

要送的报纸好像永远也送不完。巴比坐在乔的自行车后座上，一路上唧唧喳喳地讲个不停。乔试着去听，即使只用半个耳朵听也好；可是，他就是听不进去。每一次报纸砰的一声摔在人家的门廊上，他就仿佛也听到了汤尼的声音，好像在挑衅，好像在取笑："嘿！我敢打赌，你一定扔不到麦太太那些吊着的天竺葵那儿。唔，我保证，你一定扫射不到史先生的车。你怎么不干脆……"

乔很想对汤尼大吼一声，叫他闭嘴。可是，他如果真的对自己脑袋里的声音大吼大叫的话，恐怕连巴比都会认为他疯了。

为什么他要这样自责？就好像汤尼是被他推下水的？为什么他要为发生的每一件事情自责呢？要是他们当初去攀岩了，然后换成他——乔，掉下来了，汤尼一定不会这样自责。汤尼会吗？

汤尼曾说过，乔就像个老太太，总是担心这个、担心那个的。此时此刻,汤尼真应该来看看他。看到他这副模样,汤尼一定会捧腹大笑的。

想到汤尼大笑的样子,乔忍不住也微笑起来。跟汤尼在一起的日子,总是那么开心。除了这个暑假正在搭建的树屋以外,他们还有数不清的计划。

譬如说,他们正在存零用钱,准备存够了,就去买一个昆虫的养殖场。他们计划靠卖鱼饵来发财。汤尼甚至打算在暑假快结束的时候,用他妈妈的绞肉机把剩下的虫子磨碎,当做金鱼饲料来卖(因为乔的爸爸说,他们两家都不希望虫子在他们的地下室繁殖过冬)。乔虽然怀疑有谁愿意买虫子的碎末来当金鱼饲料,不过他并没有告诉汤尼他的想法。

去年暑假,他们也拟了一个很棒的赚钱计划——出售装饰用的一分钱硬币。他们把五十个一分钱硬币搁在铁轨上,让三点四十五分经过的火车压过,碾平,把每个一分钱硬币都变成了扁扁的铜片。不过,这个计划并不成功。他们总共只卖出去一个硬币。因为镇上的孩子没有一个不会这一套。他们卖出去的那一个,卖了五分钱,是卖给一个有点神经质的女孩,她妈妈根本不准她靠近铁轨。结果,剩下来四十九个卖不出去的一分钱硬币,就连口香糖球机也拒收。

乔甩出了最后一份报纸,然后调转车头,朝回家的方向骑。这时候，巴比终于安静了下来，让乔如释重负。他可以感觉到弟弟紧抓着他上衣的那双温暖小手，还有弟弟呼在他脖子后面的热气，那种感觉是那么的亲密，那么的活生生。

一股想要保护弟弟的冲动油然而生，他得快点教会巴比游泳才行。巴比现在连把脸放进水里都不敢！他得快一点带着巴比练习才行。每一个小孩都应该学会游泳的。真想不通为什么有些做父母的，好像对"这个世界有多危险"一点概念也没有！

乔转进他家旁边的街角，看到爸爸妈妈正在前面的院子里跟沙宾斯基夫妇交谈。看他们每张脸都很凝重、很急切；一股寒意直渗他的骨子里。他们在谈什么？他们已经知道了什么？大概有人已经拆穿他的谎言了吧！

或者，那个大男孩已经回到镇上供出了乔？

乔骑上车道，下了自行车，赶在巴比还没下车前，就把车子推进车库。进了车库，他才把巴比抱下来，放在地上。

"谢了，小家伙！"他说，"谢谢你的帮忙。"他把自行车靠着墙放，以免妨碍汽车出入。

"我明天还要帮你，乔！"巴比的脸在阴暗的车库里像个发光灯。

"再说吧！"乔说着拍了拍巴比的肩膀。他开始整理他的自行车，把齿轮无意义地调来调去，假装很忙的样子。

　　巴比看了他一会儿，就转过身，朝外面单脚跳了出去。"妈妈！爸爸！"他人还没出车库，就开始大叫了，"乔明天还要让我跟他一起去送报。"

　　乔默默地站着，双手不听使唤地颤抖，脸上的肌肉也近乎痉挛了。他们一定是在那边谈他。这是可想而知的。但是，他没有办法偷偷地走过他们的身边却不被看见。就算他继续待在车库里，恐怕也只会让人觉得更可疑而已。他最后又调了一次齿轮，两个肩膀低低地垂着，脸朝下，仿佛是一只很想缩回壳里的乌龟。最后，他还是走了进去，走到车道上刺眼的亮光里。

第十章　无　助

"乔,你可以过来一下吗?"乔的爸爸喊道。

乔迟疑了一下,不知道自己有没有胆量可以装作没听到。不过,他终究还是慢吞吞地转过身,头低低地朝着爸爸的叫声走过去。

"沙宾斯基家想知道你最后看到汤尼是在哪里?"爸爸问他。

乔的脑海里突然浮现汤尼哈哈大笑的画面,哗啦啦的河水正沿着他的黑发不断淌下。

"在公路上,"他说,"去饿死岩的公路上。"

"公路上的什么地方呢?"沙宾斯基先生问,"在你决定回头之前,你们两个已经骑到哪里了?"沙宾斯基先生是个大个子,有一双硕大而多毛的手。他的声音听起来显然有点不耐烦。

"噢!"乔用球鞋的前端磨烂了一朵蒲公英的花蒂,

"差不多到了那座跨河的桥吧！我想。"

"跨河的桥！"沙宾斯基太太的呼吸急促了起来。

沙宾斯基先生的身子俯向乔："可是，他说要去饿死岩州立公园的，对不对？"

"对！"乔低声地说，很懊悔一开始讲的不是原先拟好的那一套说辞。

"而且，"沙宾斯基太太说，"汤尼不会游泳。他应该知道不能去河边。"她似乎在安抚自己。

"他不会游泳？"乔歪过头、斜着眼睛看她，"真的吗？"

她浅浅地笑了一下，是乔看过无数次的那种怪怪的半笑不笑："你应该知道的，乔，你跟他一起去过游泳池……"

乔耸耸肩，眼神躲向别处。"嗯，他大部分都是在溜滑梯那里玩，要不然就是在爬绳索。可是，他从来没告诉我他不会游泳。"

沙宾斯基太太刚伸出手碰到乔的臂膀，他立刻倏地弹了开来。他觉得自己的皮肤又湿又黏，而且他相信那股河水的臭味仍然阴魂不散地跟着他。

"也许，我不应该告诉你这件事。"他说，"汤尼很可能不太想让你知道。他虽然上过几次游泳课，可还是很怕水。"

汤尼？害怕？乔简直无法接受这样的想法。

"你们还要问什么吗？"他把手插进口袋里问道。

"嗯！"他爸爸说，"我想是问完了。"乔尽量装作一副事不关己的样子走开，两只脚却差点不记得以前是怎么走路的。

他听到爸爸对沙宾斯基夫妇说："我们打个电话问一问公园的管理员。要是他不能提供什么信息，我们最好开车过去，亲自找一找。"

"我想我不应该这么担心。"沙宾斯基太太回答，"可是，你也知道汤尼这个孩子。在所有的孩子里面，最让我担心的就是他了。"

乔穿过前门，走进又黑又冷的走廊。为什么汤尼没有想到他的妈妈呢？为什么在他决定去游泳之前，没有想到她会有多么担忧呢？

乔站在莲蓬状的水龙头下，让流水洗涤他的皮肤。他已经抹了三次肥皂，一直拼命地搓洗头发和全身各处；搓好，用水冲掉，接着再抹一次。但是，水越来越冷，他没办法再耗下去了。如果再打开热水，他妈妈会生气的。

他关上水龙头，用毛巾擦干身体。在他搓着皮肤的时候，那股味道又从他的鼻孔窜了出来——那股死鱼般的河水味!

他本来想再淋浴一次,可是到底没这么做,因为再怎么洗也没用。他心里清楚得很。

他套上了睡衣睡裤,穿过黑暗的走廊,进到自己的卧室。巴比躺在床上,已经睡着了。楼下还亮着灯,爸爸妈妈低沉的交谈声从楼梯口一阵阵地飘过来。他们当然是在谈汤尼的事,他不用想也知道。

他没有打开房里的灯,就朝着床铺走过去,躺在床上,仔细地安顿好他的手、他的脚;好像不这么小心的话,就会让他痛苦不堪似的。

过了一会儿,他听到楼梯想起了轻轻的脚步声;接着,妈妈进了他的卧室,在他的床边坐下,跟他靠得那么近,她一定是假装自己没闻到他身上的臭味吧!

"乔!"她说,"你确定你已经把所有的事情都告诉我们了吗?"

"你在说什么啊?"乔故意粗鲁地回答,一副不懂妈妈在说什么的样子。其实,他心里多么期盼自己是真的不懂。

"汤尼的事啊!你们今天到底做了什么事?"

有那么一瞬间,他几乎要对她说实话了。他想,如果可以把所有的事都吐露出来,让哽塞的眼泪痛快地流下来,一定会舒坦一点。可是想到这么一来,她也得对沙宾斯基家说，对警察说；他一想到爸爸的脸上会有多么失望的表情，就什么也说不出来了。他就是说不出来。他翻过身来趴着，想用枕头掩饰自己的心绪。

"我已经告诉过你了……我累了，就先回家了。我不知道汤尼后来做了什么。"

"你们是不是吵架了？"她温和地问。

乔想起自己对汤尼发过火，却想不起来到底是为了什么事情，只清清楚楚地记得自己说了"看谁不敢！"

"没有！"他说，"我们没有吵架。"

妈妈坐着不动，好像在等他多说一点。乔只好用牙齿紧紧咬着自己的下唇。这是他唯一可以把那些快要从嘴里冲出来的话给挡回去的办法。我知道汤尼在哪里，他想说，我可以清清楚楚地告诉你要上哪里去找汤尼。

最后，妈妈弯下身来，吻了吻他的头，然后站起来走了。她离开之后，乔才放松下颌，感觉唇上火烧般的疼痛。

几分钟之后，他听到爸爸上楼的脚步声，听到爸爸在他的房外停下不动，尽力让呼吸平稳缓慢。最后，爸爸也走开了。

乔把脸埋进枕头里，让自己的鼻子和嘴深陷在窒息的黑暗中。就算他跟汤尼绑在一起攀岩，也比现在好多了。至少，他不会被孤零零地留下来。

第十一章　绝望的事实

．

　　乔默默地躺在床上等待。他怔怔地看进黑暗里,看得眼睛都痛了,仍然不肯闭上眼睛。他努力地看,努力地听,好像在等待着什么他也不知道的东西来临。

　　终于,他听见了一些声音,是汽车轮胎轻轻地摩擦着柏油路、车门开了又关,还有一些压低的说话声。他立刻站起来,走到窗前。

　　一辆汽车停在沙宾斯基家的前面,两个男人正走向他们家的前门。

　　乔的呼吸急促了起来。警察!这两个人是警察!那个大男孩还是去报案了!

　　他焦急地想把牛仔裤直接往睡裤上套,可是一双脚却被里面的布给绊住了。他只好又把牛仔裤踢开,跌跌撞撞地跑下楼。他得快点去解释清楚!千万不能让警察从沙宾斯基家那里发现他说谎……

可是，前门锁着。他花了好几秒钟才把门打开。一推开纱门，走到门口，他却裹足不前，就这么摇摇晃晃地站在台阶前。

他看见街道对面，沙宾斯基先生正侧身站在门口跟警察讲话。在沙宾斯基先生的背后，汤尼的妈妈正穿过点灯的走廊，走向前门，要加入那些人的谈话。乔的心不由得抽搐了一下。他还是慢了一步！

他转身想回屋里，可是门又开了。是爸爸一边扣着扣子，一边走了出来。乔没见到妈妈，她大概是睡着了。

"来吧！儿子，"爸爸说，"我们去看看有没有什么可以帮得上忙的。"

不！乔想低呼，更想大喊：我不要过去！可是他一个字也没吐出来。爸爸刚把手放在他的肩上，他就立刻丧失了所有的反抗力，乖乖地转过身，跟爸爸一起向沙宾斯基家走去。

"这就是和汤尼在一起的男孩。"沙宾斯基先生指着乔说。他呆板的声音听起来好像没有生命。

两名警察几乎同时转过来看乔。大大的帽沿儿让他们眼睛和嘴巴都蒙上了一层黑影。其中一名警察伸手从塑料袋里拿出汤尼那件淡蓝色的上衣。乔马上倒退了几步，可是他的手被爸爸拉住了；不知道爸爸究竟是在保护他，还是防止他逃走。

"你们发现了什么？"乔的爸爸问。

"孩子的衣服。"拎着衣服的那个警察说，"在河边。还有他的自行车。"

乔偷偷地瞅了汤尼的妈妈一眼。她用手蒙着脸，整个人不停地颤抖。她已经知道了吗？她知道他当时也在那边吗？知道他目睹了一切吗？他不敢想。

"你知道汤尼去了河边吗？"沙宾斯基先生依然用毫无生命的声音询问。

"不知道！"乔说，"我什么都不知道。我说过，我累了，所以我就……"他们全都看着他。警察、汤尼的父母，还有他爸爸，全都看着他。乔倒退了几步，但是爸爸的手再度抓住了他。虽然那双手臂只是轻轻地按在他的背上，对他来说，却像是一股沉重的压力，让他不由自主地想要挣脱，想要逃跑。要是他跑得了，他一定要躲到一个这些恐怖的眼睛再也看不到的地方。他真后悔自己没有去饿死岩。

"够了！"他说，"我说！我说！汤尼说他要去游泳的时候，我试过要阻止他。我跟他说河里很危险。"

"那么，你有没有看见他下水？"其中一个警察走近乔。

另一名警察也跟着过来，问道："当时，你在那里吗？"

"没有！"乔大喊，"没有！"

"没有人怪你，小朋友。"第一个警察说，"不过，你要是能让汤尼的父母多知道一点，"他用两只手指向沙宾斯基夫妇，好像要介绍门厅里的一幅画或是一座雕像似的，"事情就会好办得多。什么都不知道才是最让人受不了的。"

"拜托！"沙宾斯基太太低声地说，"要是你知道什么……"

沙宾斯基先生倚着门框，用他巨大的拳头紧紧地压着嘴巴，默默地饮泣。

"乔？"爸爸说，"你必须告诉我们。"他沉重的手臂压在乔的肩膀上，又转向其他人说，"乔是一个很诚实的孩子，他会告诉你们他知道的事。"

诚实？乔在爸爸沉重的手臂下晃了晃，然后挣脱开来，蹒跚地逃向门边。五张向他压过来的脸，像是五轮惨白的月亮，而其中最大的一轮，就是他爸爸的脸。

他深深吸了一口气，说道："起先汤尼说要去爬饿死岩，我很害怕，所以当他突然改变主意，说要去游泳的时候……我想……我想……"他一边说话，一边全身抖个不停。"我找过他。他沉下去的时候，我试着找过他。可是我怎么也找不到……他……他就这样……失踪了。"

"哦……乔！"这一次，爸爸的手臂不再伸向他了。"乔!"爸爸只是一再地低唤。

沙宾斯基先生呻吟着向后退进了阴暗的走廊。汤尼的母亲僵直地站着不动。她谁也不看,只是瞪着乔,一张脸恐怖地扭成一团。

每个人都在看他,在怪他。他想转身跑掉,却发现连他的脚也拒绝带他离开。他只能踉跄地走向爸爸,举起了握紧的拳头。"我恨你!"他一边嘶吼,一边猛捶着爸爸的胸膛,"都是你的错!你根本不应该让我们去的。"

爸爸没有说话,也没有抵抗,只是站在那里,默默地承受着一个又一个的拳头。直到乔自己受不了,转身跃下门廊台阶,冲过街去。

可是,就在他冲进家门,跑上楼梯,躲进房间的过程中,他心里其实一直很清楚,他恨的并不是爸爸——根本不是爸爸。

他恨的,是他自己——因为汤尼是因为他而死的。

第十二章　共同承担

　　乔蜷缩着身子侧躺在床上，眼睛直盯着房门。那是爸爸来处罚他的时候会出现的地方。他相信，这一次爸爸非处罚他不可了，再没有回旋的余地了。

　　因为，他竟敢对着爸爸大吼大叫……还拳打脚踢……因为，他竟敢怂恿汤尼和他比赛游泳到沙洲。

　　他心里始终明白这一切是自己的错。从汤尼消失的那一刻起，他就知道了。跑掉，不能改变这个事实；回家，也同样不能改变这个事实。

　　没有什么能够让已经发生的事实改变……没有！

　　夏夜的清风一阵阵地拂过他的床头，把窗外的枫树叶子吹得沙沙作响。他和汤尼的树屋就搭在那棵树上。树叶的声音和轻触着肌肤的沁凉空气，是那么的真切。能活着感受这些事物，是那么的美好。可是，汤尼再也没有机会了。汤尼再也感受不到任何事物了。

乔抬起手臂到鼻子上嗅了嗅,那味道还在,而且浓烈得让他的眼睛刺痛了起来;也许这味道就要这么跟他一辈子了。

为什么他会蠢到和汤尼打赌呢?他又不是不知道汤尼是什么样的人。就算别人和汤尼打赌从火堆上走过去,他也是不会犹豫的。

乔把枕头一会儿抓起来盖住头,一会儿又推开。他的两只眼睛就像砂纸一样又干又涩。他一心希望爸爸快点来,把一切做个了结。

前门开了又关上。乔可以听见爸爸正在锁门。难道爸爸还不了解吗?罪恶,不是可以被锁在门外的。罪恶,早在你还不知道之前就躲在你的心里了。

爸爸上楼梯了,脚步既沉重又缓慢。他照样在乔的门外停了下来。乔静静地躺着,全身肌肉绷得又紧又硬;不过,乔知道这一回装睡也没有用。

爸爸进来了,他从乔的书桌那边拉了一把椅子过来,紧挨着床边坐下。起初,他没说话。乔心想,他是不是就要这样坐一整夜?那就是他处罚我的方法!他坐在那边,我就不能逃跑,不能睡觉,甚至想哭都不能哭。

乔试着像上一回一样,尽力让呼吸平稳下来,可是他觉得自己好像跑了好长一段路,不得不喘口气。连他的皮肤也紧绷得受不了,整个人简直就要爆炸了。

"我很抱歉！"爸爸终于说话了。

"抱歉？"乔冲口而出，惊讶得翻了个身，"你抱歉什么？"

爸爸起先没有回答。乔以为他永远都不会回答的时候，他开口了："我很抱歉我误判了整个情势，我很抱歉我允许你们去。"

乔没有回应。

"而且，"爸爸继续温和地说，"我很抱歉当你需要我的时候，我没能在那里，让你一个人这么孤单、这么害怕。"

"是我的错！"乔低沉地说，"全都是我的错。"

"不！其实谁都很难在河里找到汤尼。"爸爸显然领会错了乔的意思，"而且，就算你找到了，反而会被他一起拖进水里。他比你高大、比你重，在那种情况下，他不会知道自己在干什么。"

乔回想起那淹过头部、猛灌进肺里的河水，身上登时起了一层鸡皮疙瘩。接着，他又想到了汤尼，想起汤尼宣称自己有骑施文的优先权，想起汤尼在桥上跳舞，还有装成史前怪兽的样子。"被淹死的人应该是我。"他说。

爸爸粗暴地一手抓住他的手臂："你不可以这样说！永远都不要再让我听到你这么说。"

乔直直地看着爸爸的脸。"是我害死汤尼的，"他又说，

"我要是不去河边,也许汤尼就不会下水了。"

"也许是这样,"爸爸说,"也许不是。谁都不知道。你不能靠着推测过日子。"

乔被爸爸抓着的手臂开始作痛了,可是这还不够。爸爸所说、所做的都还不够。"你要处罚我吗?"他问。

爸爸叹了口气,又沉默了半响,慢慢地放松了抓着乔的手:"这就是你想要的吗?"

"你今天早上要我用人格保证,除了公园以外,我哪里都不应该去的。"

爸爸却只问道"如果我处罚你,又能教会你什么呢?儿子……是更多的处罚吗?"

乔不知道答案,只好把脑袋里唯一的一句话说出来,而且说得粗声厉气,就像在指控罪状似的:"你的手有那个味道。"

"什么味道?"爸爸把手举到了前面。

"河水的味道。你还是没有注意到那股臭味吗?"

爸爸嗅了嗅自己的手,并弯下腰用鼻子贴近乔的皮肤闻了一下,再直起身子。

"我不懂你的意思,乔,我什么也没闻到。"

"可是我闻得到,"乔哭了起来,"它一直跟着我。"

爸爸什么也没说。

"你让它走开!"乔说得好像还有另外一个人,赖在屋里不走。

爸爸拢了拢乔脸上的头发。"我没办法！"他平静地说。

一股恨意登时让乔血脉贲张，他想把爸爸推开，再对他拳打脚踢一番。这个人有什么好的，既不能保护他不让意外发生，又不愿意处罚他来让情况变好。"你根本不懂！"他咬牙切齿地说："是我和汤尼打赌，看他敢不敢游到沙洲去。我明知道他游得不好，还故意刺激他。"

乔期待着……期待着他自己也不知道的什么东西。也许他在期待整个世界的毁灭吧！或者，至少期待爸爸会马上愤怒地站起来。可是爸爸却只是陷入长长的沉默，那种让他想要尖叫的沉默。他只好继续警戒着，等待着，不敢动弹。

"对我们两个来说，这恐怕是很难摆脱的痛苦。"爸爸最后终于开口了，"可是，我们也只能接受这个事实。"

乔坐了起来，对爸爸怒吼："你在说什么？我们？你什么也没做！你连不应该让我们去都不知道。"

"可是，我们今天都做了选择。你、我，还有汤尼。而汤尼是现在唯一不必带着悔恨过日子的人。"

片刻之间，乔瞪大了眼睛，无法理解地看着这个不愿意……不愿意替他把痛苦赶走的人。汤尼自由了，他跟爸爸却必须永远带着这个可怕的记忆过日子。即使他咬紧牙关，闭住双眼，也没有用。他忍不住啜泣起来。

"啊！"爸爸却好似松了一口气，弯下腰来，把乔拉到腿上。乔觉得有点难为情，因为他已经太大了一点；可是爸爸仍然用双手紧抱着他。他不禁把脸颊靠在爸爸的胸前，让泪水尽情地流淌。

爸爸紧抱着他，什么话也没说。过了一会儿，乔不再哭出声音，而是开始大口大口地呼吸起来。爸爸还是抱着他。又过了一会儿，乔开始跟着爸爸胸前平稳的节奏，调整自己的呼吸。

"我想睡觉了。"他终于这样说。然而，爸爸并没有立刻放下他，而是先弯下腰来把床单拉好，再站起来把他轻轻地放回床上，还替他把被子盖好。

他要离开我了。乔想，但爸爸又坐回椅子上。

乔侧着身子面对爸爸。他累了，筋疲力尽了，可是脑袋仍然很清醒。他觉得自己空荡荡的，好像内脏都被掏空了。他努力地想些话来讲，希望能听到爸爸的声音。

"你相信有天堂吗？"他终于问道，"你相信汤尼去了天堂吗？"

爸爸向乔靠过来。"如果真有天堂，我相信汤尼一定去了那里。"他回答，"我不能想象天堂会不让一个那么迷人、那么有活力的男孩进去。"

如果！乔觉得好像要沉进床里去了："你的意思到底

是什么……'如果真有天堂?'"

"我不认为有人知道,"爸爸温和地说,"死了以后会怎样。"他迟疑了一下,然后用一只手,在空中画着一连串的圈圈;画完,又把手放回腿上,好像它已经帮他做完了说明。"不过,我相信生命里有一些什么会继续存在,不会就这样在河里结束的。"

乔细细地品味着爸爸的话。他原先希望得到的是一个更明确、更清楚的答案。譬如:对!是有天堂,汤尼当然去了那里。可是,现在他必须接受他得到的答案。

此外,他还得到了一个温柔的夏夜,一个在心里永远不能填满的缺口,还有这个人——他的爸爸,坐在他床边的爸爸。

"你能陪我吗?"他伸出了一只热切的手,轻触爸爸的膝盖,"一直陪到我睡着,好吗?"

"当然!"爸爸坚定地说。

On My Honor

Marion Dane Bauer

For the Mason family,

whose lives formed

part of the fabric of my childhood.

Chapter 1

"Climb the Starved Rock Bluffs? You've gotta be kidding!" Joel's spine tingled at the mere thought of trying to scale the sheer river bluffs in the state park. He looked Tony square in the eye. "Somebody got killed last year trying to do that! Don't you remember?"

Tony shrugged, popped a wheelie on his battered BMX, spun in place. "Nobody knows if that guy was really trying to climb the bluffs. He might have fallen off the top...or even jumped."

Joel bent over his Schwinn ten-speed and brushed imaginary dust off the fender. "Well, I'm not going to ride out there with you if that's what you're going to do. It's dumb." He tried to sound tough, sure of himself. Maybe, for once, he would be able to talk Tony out of one of his crazy ideas.

"You don't have to climb if you're scared, Bates," Tony said.

"Who's scared?" Joel licked his lips, which seemed to have gone dry. "I'd just rather go swimming, that's all. It's going to be a scorcher today. Or we could work on our tree house. My dad got us some more wood."

"We can do the tree house later," Tony said, "after we get back. And I don't feel like swimming."

"You never feel like swimming," Joel muttered, seeing in his mind the shining blue water of the municipal pool. The truth was, Tony rarely felt like doing anything that Joel wanted to do. Joel wondered, sometimes, why they stayed friends. There had to be something more than their having been born across the street from each other twelve years ago, their birthdays less than a week apart.

Mrs. Zabrinsky, Tony's mother, started babysitting Joel after his mother went back to work when he was six months old, so he and Tony had spent their baby years drooling on the same toys. Now Joel just checked in with her during the day, let her know where he was going, things like that. But he didn't know what kept him and Tony together except that, after Tony, other kids seemed boring.

"Come on, Joel," Tony said. "Ride out to the park with

me today, and tomorrow I'll go swimming with you."

Joel thought of the long, curving, watery slide at the pool. He sighed. Tomorrow it would probably rain. Or Tony would have some other plan...as crazy as this one. He would pretend he had forgotten he promised to go to the pool. Joel resettled his lunch in the saddlebag behind his bicycle seat. It wasn't much fun to go swimming alone, but still it would be better than getting killed on the park bluffs. There were signs all over warning people to stay on the paths, and Tony wanted to climb from the river side, no less.

The front door of Joel's house opened and his father came out with Bobby, Joel's four-year-old brother. Mrs. Zabrinsky was Bobby's baby-sitter now, and their father was always the one to give Bobby his breakfast and take him to the Zabrinskys' house because their mother had to leave for work earlier than he.

Seeing his father and the firm grip he maintained on Bobby's hand gave Joel an idea. He would ask for permission to ride his bike out to Starved Rock. He wouldn't mention about the bluffs, of course. He wouldn't have to. His father was sure to say that the ride to the park was too far, too dangerous. His dad always worried about things like that. Tony would be mad that he had asked, but they were *supposed* to ask, after all. At least Tony wouldn't be able to say that Joel had stayed home because he was chicken.

"Hi, Dad," Joel called. This was going to be easy. "Can I bike out to Starved Rock with Tony?" He turned his back slightly to Tony to avoid seeing what he knew would be a dirty look.

His father stopped and squinted against the morning sun that had just risen above the houses across the street. "All the way out to the state park?" he repeated, as though there were some other Starved Rock in Illinois.

"Yeah," Joel said. "It's not so far. Probably only ten or twelve miles."

"More like eight or nine, I think," his father said, approaching with Bobby in tow, "but it's still a long ride."

"I wanna go, too," Bobby announced. "I wanna go to the park. Can I, Daddy? Can I, Joel?" His voice reminded Joel of the hovering whine of a mosquito. Their mother said whining was a stage all four-year-olds went through. Joel thought a year was a long stage.

"It's a hot day," his father continued, ignoring Bobby's plea, "and that road is awfully narrow…hilly and winding, too."

"Can I, Daddy?" Bobby's voice rose in volume and pitch. "Can I go with Joel?"

"No." Their father shook his head. "I'm not even sure these two are going anywhere. Now, you run across to the Zabrinskys. But be careful, Bobby! Watch for cars!"

There were almost no cars to watch for on their quiet street, but their father always said things like that anyway. Bobby went, his lower lip sticking out like a shelf.

"We'll be careful, Dad," Joel could hear the whine in his own voice. He sounded almost as bad as Bobby. He sounded as if he really wanted to go.

"We will, Mr. Bates. Honest!" Tony pleaded. "The park's not that far...and there's not much traffic during the week."

Joel's father ran his fingers through his hair, leaving it standing on end. "I know the traffic is sparse, but with all those hills...it'll seem like a lot farther."

"If we get tired, we'll just turn back," Tony said.

Joel didn't say anything more. To win this argument would be to lose. He was sure, though, that his father wasn't going to give permission.

His father surveyed their bikes, frowning slightly. Joel wondered if he was going to ask why Tony was carrying a rope looped over his handlebars. *To tie ourselves together when we climb*, Tony had announced. But Joel's father merely said, "You have lunches packed already?"

"Sure," Tony answered, patting the lunch he had tied to his handlebars with the rope.

Joel's father turned back to him. "You know you have your paper route to do this afternoon, Joel."

Joel nodded. He knew. Maybe *that* would be an excuse.

"What if you boys get too tired to ride back? Tony's mother doesn't have a car, and I don't want anybody to have to leave work to come after you."

Tony was looking at Joel, obviously waiting for him to play out his side of the argument.

"We won't get tired," Joel said automatically.

His father's eyes seemed to know better, but he turned to Tony and asked, "Does your mother know what you're planning to do?"

"Sure," Tony answered cheerfully, and Joel knew, without even checking Tony's face, that he was lying. He never told his mother anything if he could help it, and she was so busy with the littler kids that she didn't ask many questions.

His father merely accepted Tony's word with a nod—

grown-ups could be really dense sometimes—but then he almost redeemed himself by suggesting, "How about trying the county road that goes out of town the other way? It's flat and would be easier riding."

"It doesn't go anywhere," Tony complained. "Besides, it's boring. Nothing but cornfields on every side."

No bluffs to climb, Joel added silently.

Joel's father sighed, buttoned his suit jacket, and then unbuttoned it again. The sigh gave Joel's stomach a small twist. His father wasn't actually considering giving permission, was he? Tony's father would have answered in a second. He would have said, "No!"

"What do you think, son?" his father asked. "Do you really think you can make it all the way to the park and back without any trouble?"

Joel could feel Tony watching him, waiting. "Sure," he said, though his throat seemed to tighten around the word. "It'll be a cinch."

Joel's father shook his head. "I doubt that, but I guess it won't hurt you boys to be good and tired tonight."

Joel's knees went watery. His father was going to say they could go!

"We'll build up the muscles in our legs," Tony announced,

jubilant.

Joel's father didn't take his eyes off Joel's face. "On your honor?" he said. "You'll watch for traffic, and you won't go anywhere except the park? You'll be careful the whole way?"

"On my honor," Joel repeated, and he crossed his heart, solemnly, then raised his right hand. To himself, he added, *The only thing I'll do is get killed on the bluffs, and it'll serve you right.*

His father looked at him for a long moment; then he nodded his head. "Okay," he said. "I guess you're old enough now for a jaunt like this."

"Put her there, man," Tony exclaimed, holding a grubby palm toward Joel, and then he added, "I get dibs on the Schwinn!"

Joel gave Tony five, taking in his friend's face as he did. Tony's dark eyes were bright with laughter, with fun, and he was grinning like a circus clown. Joel shook his head. "How can you get dibs on *my* bike?" he asked, though he knew how. When you were Tony, the outrageous seemed natural.

His father was still watching him, so Joel added, automatically, "Thanks, Dad." He tried to sound as though he were really glad. He even forced a smile, though his mouth felt stiff. "Thanks a lot."

His father nodded again, his face remaining serious. "Remember, son," he said one last time, "you're on your honor."

"Sure," Joel replied. The least his father could have done was to remind them about staying off the bluffs. "I know."

Chapter 2

Joel watched his father drive away. He felt betrayed, trapped. How could he explain to Tony that he had been kidding, that he had never had any intention of going with him to the park once the idea of climbing the bluffs had comp up?

"Can I ride your bike, Joel?" Tony begged. "Can I, huh?"

Joel sighed. Tony was like a kid expecting Christmas, not someone about to risk his life. "Just for the ride out," he said. When they came back—*if* they came back—he knew he would be glad for the gears on the Schwinn to make the ride easier.

Tony's bike was a hand-me-down that had belonged to three older brothers before it had come to be his. There were no fenders, no handlegrips, and only a few flecks left of the original red paint. It was perfect for wheelies, though, and for going off ramps. Joel's silver ten-speed could be ridden fast or it could be ridden slowly, but it wasn't good for anything else.

Joel reached over to take hold of Tony's bike, supporting his own for Tony at the same time. "Come on," he said. "Let's go."

It took only about ten minutes to reach the edge of town. On their way past the school, Tony stuck out his tongue in the direction of the sixth grade classroom where they had spent last year. Joel, deciding he might as well get into the spirit of the day, followed suit, though he liked school well enough.

The sun sizzled in a sky so blue it could have been created out of a paint can. When they left the town behind, they rode between stands of tall, whispering grass rising on each side of the highway. Meadowlarks called from the ditch banks.

Tony's exuberance knew no bounds. He rode in figure eights or in circles that occupied both lanes of the nearly deserted highway. Once he tried a square and nearly toppled off Joel's bike.

Joel moved ahead, and when he started down the hill

into the Vermillion River valley, he leaned forward and pumped, pushing Tony's old bike until it hummed. This was the first of many valleys they would encounter, and Joel knew going up the other side would be tough. Maybe, he thought, with a sudden rush of hope, Tony would get tired before they got all the way to the park.

Soon the bike was going faster than he could pump, so he had to let it coast. Still it gathered speed. He tried, once, to glance over his shoulder to see how close behind Tony was following. His front wheel wobbled dangerously when he turned his head, though, so he kept his eyes forward, concentrating on keeping the wheel still. His tires buzzed against the smooth blacktop, and the wind swept through his hair, holding it back from his face as if by strong fingers. It forced his eyelids open and made his eyes feel dry and crackly.

By the time Joel got to the bridge, the lowest point between the two hills, he would be flying. With the speed he had built up, he figured he could be halfway up the other side before he had to get off to push.

Joel reached the bottom of the hill and shot across the bridge so fast that he didn't get even a glimpse of the river below. He knew exactly how it would look, though, muddy red with lazy, oilylooking swirls. As soon as the bike's momentum slowed enough that his legs could keep pace with the spinning wheels, he started pumping, measuring his distance on the upward side, standing when the pumping began to get hard so he could force each pedal down with all his weight.

When his legs began to feel rubbery, he climbed off and started pushing. Tony would probably pass him, still riding the Schwinn.

"That was some hill, huh?" He tossed the words over his shoulder. Getting no answer, he turned around to see where Tony was.

Tony was at the bottom of the hill in the middle of the bridge, the Schwinn leaning carelessly against the fat iron railing. He was hanging a long way out over the railing, peering down at the river.

"Bummer!" Joel said and, glancing up and down the highway to check for cars—even when he was mad at his father he couldn't help doing things like that—he U-turned, climbed back on, and began coasting again. Next time he wouldn't get more than a few feet trying to start up from a dead stop at the bottom. He would have to walk the entire hill. But of course Tony didn't think of things like that. Maybe it was time they trade bikes back again.

"What're you looking at?" he asked, as he popped a wheelie and spun next to Tony.

"The river," Tony replied, leaning out even farther. "I'm looking at Old Man River."

"No, you're not. Old Man River is the Mississippi. That's nothing but the Vermillion down there."

Tony didn't answer. Joel knew his correction didn't matter to Tony. If he wanted to call the Vermillion Old Man River, he would. He was that way in school, too...even on tests. He drove the teachers nuts.

Looking at Tony leaning over the railing like some kind of acrobat on a trapeze, Joel suddenly had to turn away. He wished Tony would be more careful.

Beyond all reason he also wished, as he often had before, that Tony were his brother. They could be twins...the kind that didn't have to look alike or *be* alike either. With so many other kids in the family, the Zabrinskys wouldn't miss Tony. If they needed a replacement, Joel would gladly trade Bobby-the-Whiner.

"You realize," Joel said, "that it's going to be a long walk up that hill."

Tony straightened up and grinned, his teeth bright

against his already tanned skin. "We don't *have* to go to Starved Rock," he said. "Maybe I've got a better idea."

"Better than Starved Rock?" Was there a chance he wasn't going to have to argue with Tony about climbing the bluffs?

Tony did a little jig next to the bridge railing as if he could explain himself that way. "We've got lots of time. We can do anything we want."

"Sure we can!" Joel agreed enthusiastically.

"We could even go swimming."

Joel couldn't believe his luck. "All *right!*" he exclaimed, holding out the flat of his palm for Tony to slap.

Tony ignored the gesture and instead bowed, extending a hand in the direction of the reddish brown water slithering far beneath the bridge. "It's a great day for swimming," he said.

Joel stared. "In the river?" he demanded. "You want to go swimming in the river?"

Tony shrugged elaborately. "Where else?"

"You might as well go swimming in your toilet."

"Who says?"

"My dad says! That's who."

"'My dad says,'" Tony mimicked, his voice coming out

high and girlish.

Joel decided to ignore the taunt. He decided, also, not to remind Tony of the promise he had been required to make to his father before they left. "You know we're not allowed to swim in the Vermillion. Nobody is. It's dangerous...sink holes and currents. Whirlpools, sometimes! Besides being dirty."

"Alligators, too, I bet." Tony was suddenly solemn, though his eyes still danced. "The red in the water probably comes from all the bloody pieces of swimmers the 'gators leave lying around."

"There's no alligators in the Vermillion! Do you think I'm stupid or something?" Joel could feel his face growing hot, despite the fact that he knew Tony was only teasing. "And the color just comes from clay, red clay."

"That does it!" Tony said, crossing his arms and pulling his T-shirt over his head. "If there's no 'gators and no blood, I'm going swimming for sure."

Leaving Joel's Schwinn still perched haphazardly against the railing, he went whooping the length of the bridge and crashed through the underbrush along the side of the road. He was swinging his pale blue shirt over his head like a lasso.

"Come on, Joel," he yelled back. "The last one in's a two-toed sloth!"

Chapter 3

Joel watched Tony yelling and flailing his arms as he ran down the steep hill to the river. He shook his head. That patch of shiny green leaves halfway down that Tony was romping through was probably poison ivy.

He glanced over at his bike. Tony hadn't even bothered to hide it in the weeds along the side of the road. Joel propped Tony's old bike against the railing and wheeled his own off the bridge, laying it gently in the weeds beneath the structure. He considered, for a moment, leaving Tony's bike right where Tony had left his, out in the open where anybody could steal it. He didn't, though. If Tony's bike got stolen, he might never get another.

Swimming in the Vermillion! Of all the crazy ideas! Maybe even crazier than climbing the bluffs. Joel shook his head as he laid Tony's bike next to his own; then he started down the hill.

"You see what I mean?" Joel said when he arrived next to Tony on the riverbank. "It's really dirty. And the worst of the stuff, chemicals and sewage, you can't even see."

Tony ignored him, stripping off his jeans and his underwear. He had already dropped his shirt and kicked his sneakers off before Joel arrived. "It's wet, isn't it?" he asked.

"Like I said," Joel replied, "so's your toilet."

Tony stepped into the river at the edge, and the dirty water lapping over his feet made them disappear entirely. He turned back to Joel and grinned. "Not enough water in my toilet. I tried it once to see."

"You would," Joel replied. He wanted to sound grumpy, but he could feel the answering smile breaking through.

"You coming in?" Tony called back when the water swirled around his knees.

"I'm waiting for you to drown," Joel answered. "I just want to see it so I can tell your folks."

"Keep them from worrying," Tony tossed back. "Keep your mom from waiting supper," Joel replied.

They both laughed then, and when the laughter had

faded, Tony said, "Well, are you coming in, or are you just going to stand there and gawk?"

"Who's gawking?" Joel pushed one sneaker off with the toe of the other. "You're nothing to look at."

The water was just right, cool enough to raise gooseflesh at first but not cold enough to be numbing. The flow past Joel's legs felt like a refreshing massage. He hadn't realized, though, that the current was so strong. It seemed as though the water were barely moving when he looked down from the bridge.

"Watch out for the current," he called to Tony, standing several feet upriver from him.

"Agh!" Tony cried, grasping himself by the throat with both hands. "The current! It's got me. It's going to suck me under. It's going to swallow me up!" And he toppled over backward, howling. His head disappeared beneath the foaming water he churned up.

Joel stood where he was, waiting. When Tony stood up, he was a prehistoric monster emerging from a swamp. Joel could tell that was what he was by the way he stood, water streaming down his face, arms hanging low, head hunched forward.

"Come on," Joel said. "If we're going to swim, let's go back to the pool. It'll be better there."

Tony straightened up. "Why? This is fun!"

"But there's a sliding board at the pool. And there's other kids, too."

"Who needs a sliding board...or other kids?" Tony replied. "Besides, I'm swimming now." And he plunged into the water, face first this time, but thrashing just as much as before.

"Doesn't look like he even knows how," Joel muttered to himself, but then he wiped away the idea. It seemed disloyal. Tony went to the pool with him now and then, and he did the same things everybody else did. They spent most of their time going down the slide into shallow water or splashing one another.

Joel eased himself deeper into the water and dog-paddled a few strokes. He didn't want to put his face down to swim properly. He'd take the artificial blue of a pool and the sting of the chlorine any day. The river smelled of decaying fish.

"Maybe we ought to come down here every day, work out. We could be on the swim team next year in junior high," Tony was saying.

Joel stopped trying to swim and stood up. "We'd get caught for sure if we started coming down here every day."

"Who's to see us?" Tony asked.

"I don't know, but somebody would. Somebody driving over the bridge, probably." Joel looked up toward the highway bridge, but there were no cars in sight.

Tony shook his head. "Sometimes, Bates, you sound just like your old man."

Joel could feel the head flooding his face. "What's wrong with that?"

"'Be careful in that tree, son,'" Tony mimicked, "'you might get hurt. Watch Bobby when he crosses the street. Those drivers never pay any—'"

Joel had been moving closer to Tony as he spoke, and now he gave him a hard shove. Tony was expecting it, though, and he didn't even step backward. He countered with a push of his own.

Joel swung his arms to keep his balance, and he felt the bubble of anger that had been with him all morning expand inside his chest. What right did Tony have to make fun of his father? "At least my dad doesn't go around hitting kids with a belt," he said, stepping closer to Tony and clenching his fists.

Tony went white around the mouth, and Joel was instantly sorry that he had picked on Tony's father. He didn't know that Mr. Zabrinsky had ever really hit Tony with a belt anyway. He had only seen him take off after Tony once, snaking his belt out through the loops with one hand and holding his pants up with the other. Actually, Joel had thought it was kind of funny at the time…in a scary sort of way.

Tony took a wide swing at the side of Joel's head. Joel ducked it easily. Tony was bigger and heavier than he was, but he was slower, too.

For a moment they stood glowering at one another, breathing hard, their fists raised; then Tony turned and began to slog through the water toward the riverbank.

"Where are you going?" Joel asked.

"To Starved Rock," came the reply. "I'm gonna climb the bluffs…by myself."

Joel's heart sank. He didn't especially want to bike back to town alone, and he certainly didn't want Tony climbing the bluffs by himself. "Aw, come on, Tony," he pleaded. "We can stay here. This is fun."

"Like swimming in your toilet," Tony replied without looking back.

Joel answered with the first thing that popped into his head—"Toilets aren't so bad"—and to show Tony that he meant it, he plunged into the water, immersing his face and taking several strokes so that when he stood up he was in front of Tony again.

Tony grunted. He still looked pretty mad. "You're just saying that because you're scared to climb the bluffs."

Again the irritation flared. "Who's scared?" Joel demanded. "You're the one who's scared. Why, I bet you wouldn't even"—he hesitated, looking around for something to challenge Tony with, something he wouldn't mind doing himself—"swim to that sandbar out there." He indicated a thin, dark island of sand rising out of the river about a hundred feet from where they stood.

Tony narrowed his eyes, gazed in the direction Joel pointed. "Why should I be scared of that?" he asked scornfully. "I'll bet the river doesn't get deeper than this the whole way." The water divided at Tony's waist in a sharp V.

"I'll bet it's deeper than this lots of places," Joel said. "River bottoms change. That's one of the reasons they're so dangerous."

"I wouldn't be scared even if it was ten foot deep."

Joel steeped closer. "You willing to swim it then?"

Tony's chin shot up. "Sure. Unless you're too chicken to swim it, too."

"We'll see who's chicken, " Joel said.

Chapter 4

Joel pushed off with a breast stroke. After a few of those and a couple more dog paddles, he gave up and put his face down so he could swim properly. He kept his eyes closed underwater, though. Every few strokes he raised his head, glanced toward the sandbar, and realigned himself. The current was pushing him downstream, and if he wasn't careful he would miss the sandbar entirely.

He could hear Tony splashing wildly behind him, puffing and spewing water, his hands flailing. He couldn't figure out why he had never noticed what a poor swimmer Tony was before now.

Joel touched bottom for a moment to catch his breath, peering back toward the riverbank, wiping the water from his face and trying to forget how dirty it was. Tony came to an agitated stop behind him, and Joel faced him. "If you can't swim any better than that, you'll never make the swim team next year."

Tony's chest was heaving. He gasped for breath as if he had been swimming for miles. "That's why I want to work out every day. You and me. I'll get better. We both will."

"How about working out at the pool?" Joel asked, feeling reasonable and somehow older than Tony, the way he often did. "It's cleaner, and we won't get into trouble for going there."

"How about working out in the middle of Main Street?" Tony replied. "Then everybody can see." He was still breathing hard.

"What difference does it make if anybody sees?"

"All the difference in the world. Do you want Rundle and Schmitt noticing what we're doing? If they see, then they'll want to try out for the team, too."

"So...let them try out. Who cares?" Joel couldn't figure out what was going on. This wasn't like Tony. He was always everybody's friend. So much so that sometimes Joel couldn't help but feel a little bit jealous, wanting to keep Tony to himself.

Maybe Tony knew his form was bad, and he was embarrassed. He'd probably never had lessons at the Y like most of the kids, and the last thing in the world he was ever willing to do was admit that there was something he didn't know.

Joel could still remember the time Tony had claimed to be an expert at hang gliding. He'd jumped out of his upstairs window with a sheet tied to his wrists and ankles. Tony said, afterward, that the reason it hadn't worked was because he hadn't jumped from high enough. The doctor had said Tony was lucky to have gotten off with only a broken arm.

"Come on," Tony prodded. "You said out to the sandbar. Are you giving up?"

"You sure you'll make it?" Joel eyed his friend's still faintly heaving chest meaningfully. "You look pretty tired to me."

Tony gave him a shove, almost caught him off balance. "Swim," he commanded, and Joel plunged into the water and resumed swimming. Tony started beside him but immediately dropped behind. Joel could hear him, blowing and puffing like a whale.

It's not so bad, Joel said to himself, beginning to get his rhythm, discovering the angle that made it possible to keep gaining against the current. Maybe Tony was right and this river swimming would be a good way to practice...now that his father had decided he was old enough to be allowed a bit of freedom.

He started the side stroke. He could watch where he was going better that way, keep tabs on how far he still had to go. He couldn't see Tony coming behind, but he didn't need to see him. He could tell he was there, because he sounded like an old paddle wheeler.

Only about twenty more feet. Joel caught a toehold in the bottom for a second to look ahead. The water foamed and eddied around the sandbar as if it were in more of a hurry there than other places. He put his head down and began the crawl, angling upriver against the current.

He was gasping for breath each time he turned his head. He wasn't really tired, though. A little nervous, maybe. In the pool the side was always nearby, something to grab on to. Still, he was a pretty good swimmer, and he was doing all right. He *might* be good enough for the swim team by the time he got to junior high in the fall.

He should have thought of practicing in the river himself. It had been a good idea. Tony was full of good ideas. When they both reached the sandbar, he would apologize, tell Tony he was sorry for what he'd said about his dad. He'd tell him he was sorry about saying Tony would be afraid to swim a little ways, too.

"Made it," he called out, when his hand scraped bottom with his approach to the sandbar. He stood up. "And I beat you, too!"

There was no answer. Joel turned to check.

Behind him stretched the river, smooth and glistening, reddish brown, but there was no sign of Tony. There was nothing to indicate that Joel wasn't alone, hadn't come into the water alone to start with. Except, of course, he hadn't.

He started to walk back, pushing through the water impatiently, as though it were a crowd holding him back. "Tony," he yelled. "Where are you?"

A faint echo of his own voice, high like the indistinct mewing of a cat, bounced back at him from the bluffs, but there was no other reply. Joel kept walking forward, pushing against the wall of water.

Maybe Tony had turned back; maybe he was hiding in the bushes somewhere along the bank, watching him, waiting for him to come unglued.

"All right, Tony Zabrinsky. I know your tricks. Come out, wherever you are."

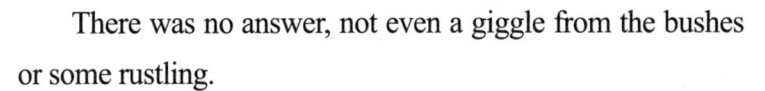

There was no answer, not even a giggle from the bushes or some rustling.

"Doggone you, Tony, if you mess with my clothes…" But he could see his clothes, the pile of them, lying where he had left them, his red T-shirt marking the spot.

"Tony!" He began to move forward in lunges, gasping for breath, half choking. Tony had to be hiding. He had to be just off to the side somewhere…laughing. There was no other possibility.

It was when Joel stepped off into the nothingness of the deep water, the river bottom suddenly gone from beneath his feet as if he had hit a black hole in space, that he knew. As he choked and fought his way to the surface, he understood everything.

Tony couldn't swim—not really—and Tony had gone under.

Chapter 5

Joel treaded water for another few seconds, looking across the deceptively smooth surface of the river. There was nothing there, no faint difference in the appearance of the water, nothing to give a hint of danger. How wide across was the hole? Where did Tony go under? Would he still be where he went down, or would the current have carried him away by now? How long could a person be underwater and still live?

The questions came at Joel in a barrage, leaving no space for answers, if there were any answers.

There wasn't time to wait for them anyway. He made a lunging dive, pulling himself forward and under with both arms, his eyes open and smarting in the murky water. He couldn't see more than a few inches in front of his face, so he reached in every direction with his hands as he swam, feeling for an arm, a leg, a bit of hair. Anything! He found nothing until he touched something slimy and rotting on the bottom and sprang to the surface.

He ducked under the water again, reaching on every side, looking and feeling until the river sang in his ears and he burst through to the light, pulling raggedly for air.

The current would have pulled Tony downstream. He let the river carry him a few feet farther on and tried again.

Nothing.

When Joel dove for the fourth time, letting the current carry him farther from the shore, he found himself caught in the grip of that hurrying water. It sucked at him, grinding him against the silty river bottom. As he struggled to rise, grasping at the water with both hands as if he could pull himself up by it, his hand touched something solid.

Was it Tony, floating just above him? He thrashed toward the object, only to have the current draw it from his reach. Then he was swirling, spinning, being pulled toward the bottom again while a dark, boy-shaped object pivoted above him, facedown in the muddy water.

Tony was dead...dead! And he, Joel, was going to die, too. He couldn't breathe. His lungs were a sharp pain. The air came bursting from his chest like an explosion, and the water rushed in to take its place. The form that had ridden above him brushed against his arm, his side. It was rough, hard, no human body. It was a log. Joel grabbed hold, and his head broke through the light-dazzled surface just as the rest of his body gave in to limpness.

He lay for a few minutes, coughing, spitting water, being moved without any assistance on his part from the eddying whirlpool to the slower, straighter current close to the riverbank. When the river bottom came up to meet his feet, he stood.

The sky was an inverted china bowl above his head. A single bird sang from a nearby tree.

Shut up, Joel wanted to shout. *You just shut up*. But he didn't. He didn't say anything. Instead, he bent over double and vomited a stream of water. Strange that river water in small amounts looked clean.

Joel could see everything with a sharp, terrible clarity: the river water he vomited, the bare roots of a tree thrust above the water, the steady progress of the river toward… where did it go? Toward the Illinois River. And the Illinois River emptied into the Mississippi. Didn't it?

They had studied rivers in school, but he couldn't remember.

He looked around. Still nothing disturbed the smooth surface of the water, and nothing skulked along the bank, no hidden form. He might have been the only human being alive in the entire world.

If he found Tony, if he found him hiding somewhere on the bank, he would beat him to a bloody pulp. He would never speak to him again, never do anything with him again. It was a dirty trick, the dirtiest trick Tony had ever pulled.

A shiver convulsed Joel, though the sun was still bright and hot, and he began to move woodenly toward the spot where he had left his clothes. He would get dressed and—

He stood there over his pile of clothes. Tony's clothes were scattered on the ground, exactly where he had dropped them. Tony couldn't have gotten out of the water. Not even Tony would be running around stark naked... just for a joke! Joel turned back to face the river again, squinting against the sunlight that glinted off the rippling surface.

It wasn't possible. It couldn't be. It was all a terrible dream from which he would awaken any moment.

Far above him, a car rumbled across the bridge.

"Wait!" Joel screamed, coming out of the trance in which he had been standing over Tony's clothes. "Stop! Help!" He ran toward the bridge, flailing his arms, but the car was too far away for anyone to hear...to see. It moved smoothly up the hill on the other side of the bridge.

Joel stopped in his tracks, trembling, his teeth chattering in erratic bursts, then ran back to his clothes. He grabbed his jeans from the pile, letting his underpants and shirt tumble to the ground. His hands shook so violently that he could barely hold the jeans up to step into them. The heavy material stuck against his wet skin. He tried to stuff his feet into his sneakers, gave up, and began to run toward the highway, still struggling to fasten the jeans. There would be another car coming soon. There had to be.

As he ran, he paid no attention to where he stepped. He looked down once, after tripping and picking himself up, to see that his big toe was bleeding, but it might have been someone else's toe. He felt nothing. A thistle beneath his left foot only made him move faster...up the hill, his lungs pumping. The air seemed to hold him back exactly as the water had earlier.

By the side of the highway, he doubled over, vomited again, and then stood erect. He had to get help. Maybe Tony could still be saved if he got help. The road climbed away from the river on each side...empty...bare. There wasn't a single car or truck in view. The only movement anywhere was a black crow wheeling high in the sky.

Joel turned toward home and began to run blindly up the middle of the highway. He could feel the river just behind him, a presence, a lurking monster waiting to pounce. A monster that swallowed boys. Joel increased his speed, his heart hammering against his ribs, his bare feet slapping against the dark pavement.

Chapter 6

Joel was halfway up the hill before another car crested the rise at the top and started toward him. It was a big, old boat of a car, blue with silver fenders, a red and orange flame painted on the hood. Joel planted himself in the middle of the lane, waving his arms. The blue car swerved toward the opposite side of the road, and he lunged to stay in its path, determined not to let it get away. The car came to a screeching, vibrating halt, inches from his extended arms.

"What in the hell do you think you're doing?" the driver yelled. He was a teenage boy, probably eighteen or nineteen, with a lot of dark hair and bare, muscular arms.

"Please," Joel gasped, but then he couldn't say any more. He stood doubled over the car's hood, trying to catch his breath, trying to get the words past his throat. "Please," he repeated.

"The kid looks sick," a blonde girl said. She was sitting next to the boy, so close that she could have been sharing the driving. She leaned forward as she spoke, peering through the windshield at Joel.

"In the river," he managed to say, pointing. "Please, come."

"What's in the river?" the boy asked, attentive now. "What're you talking about?"

Joel shook his head, unable to speak again. His face felt numb.

"You mean somebody's drowning or something?" The boy leaned forward, gripping the wheel.

Joel nodded dumbly.

"Get in!" the driver ordered, reaching back and swinging the door open for Joel.

Joel stumbled around the car and slid into the backseat, pulling the door shut again. The blonde girl turned and stared, her mouth working methodically around a wad of purple gum. She looked scared.

The car started up with a screeching of tires, barreled down the road, and skidded to a stop on the gravel shoulder just before the bridge.

"Who'd you say it is?" the boy demanded, already

out of the car and jerking open Joel's door. "A friend of yours?"

"Yeah," Joel said, finding a bit of voice as he climbed out of the car. "His name's Tony."

"Where'd he go in?"

"I'll show you," Joel said, and he headed for the riverbank at a stumbling run. The bigger boy ran beside him, the girl next to the boy, her hands fluttering in front of her like large moths.

The sight of the river, the faint, dead-fish smell of it, made Joel's knees buckle when he got to the bank again. The boy grabbed his arm and held him up.

"Here?" he asked, setting Joel back on his feet.

"There's a place where it gets deep…right about there." Joel pointed in the direction of the spot where he thought Tony had gone down.

The boy pulled off his shirt. "How'd he get in there anyway?" he asked.

"We were swimming out to the sandbar, and when I looked back…he wasn't there. I…I tried to find him. I really did." Joel choked as he spoke, his chest heaving in something like a sob, but he wasn't crying. His eyes were perfectly dry, and though he was shaking, his insides were frozen into a dead calm.

The boy had kicked off his shoes and his jeans. He stepped into the river, then paused, squinting at the muddy water.

"This his clothes?" the girl asked, approaching with Tony's blue shirt cradled in her arms as if she thought she had rescued Tony.

"Yeah," Joel answered, resisting an impulse to tell her to keep her hands off Tony's things.

The boy plunged into the water, skimming beneath the surface, humping up and diving more deeply still.

"You be careful," the girl called toward the place where her boyfriend had disappeared.

Joel and the girl stood side by side, waiting. Joel wondered for a moment if he should be back in the water looking, too, but the memory of the current pulling at him, holding him down, turned his legs to lead. He couldn't move toward the river again. The boy was going to find Tony, anyway. Joel was certain of it.

The first time the boy surfaced, Joel called out excitedly…"Tony!" But the teenager's hands were empty, and Joel stifled a second, more forlorn cry.

"The current probably took him that way,"Joel called,

pointing toward the bridge, and the boy nodded and ducked under again, swimming farther out this time and emerging downriver ten or fifteen feet.

He stayed with it, turning in every direction, diving again and again until his chest heaved and he staggered when he stood. His girl friend paced on the bank, cracking her gum steadily. "Be careful. Be careful," she said occasionally, more to the surrounding air than to her friend.

"You won't find anything there," she called desperately when he swam almost to the middle of the river once. "He wouldn't have gone that far out."

"But what if he did?" Joel demanded, and the girl didn't answer. She looked as though she were about to cry.

Joel stood on the bank and called helpful directions, but finally, despite Joel's encouraging suggestion to try "just a bit farther down," the boy began wading toward shore. His head was lowered so the water sheeting off his hair wouldn't drip into his eyes.

"You aren't quitting, are you?" Joel asked, the knowledge that he had quit already lying heavily in his gut.

"Yeah," the boy gasped, picking up his shirt and wiping his face with it. "I'm quitting."

"But you can't," Joel waited. "You just can't!"

The boy shrugged. He spoke between deep, quavering breaths. "Look...do you know...how long...it takes somebody...to drown?"

Joel didn't answer. He hadn't thought about it. Besides, he didn't want to know.

"About five minutes, I'd say." The boy bent over, resting his hands on his knees. "About five lousy minutes!" More deep breaths. "Maybe even less."

Joel turned away, walked along the bank a few feet, but the boy's voice followed him.

The boy was beginning to breathe more normally now, and the words came out in large clumps. "And how long was it before you even got me down here? Ten minutes? Fifteen?"

Joel couldn't respond.

"And do you know," the boy went on, straightening up slowly, "how hard it to find anything in a river like this... how fast the current would pull somebody along? Maybe next week a body'll wash up at one of the dams...or next month."

"We're not looking for a body," Joel said, turning back fiercely. "It's Tony we're looking for!"

The boy used his shirt to shear the water off his chest

and arms. He shook his head. "Sorry, kid," he said.

Joel went rigid. What was this guy saying? Sorry? What was he sorry about? He didn't even know Tony.

"Dumb kids," the boy muttered as he tugged on his jeans. "You shouldn't have been swimming in the river in the first place. You both should have known better. Didn't anybody ever tell you how dangerous rivers are?" He stuffed his feet into his shoes, wrung his wet shirt out. "Well," he said, "you'd better finish getting dressed and come with me."

Now it was Joel who was beginning to have trouble breathing. "Where are you going?" he asked.

"To the police station." The boy's voice was harsh, angry, as if he blamed Joel for what had happened. "When somebody drowns, you've got to report it to the police."

When somebody drowns. The words reverberated through Joel's skull like a scream. But he only repeated, dully, "The police," and stared at his own feet. What would the police say? They would want to know what Joel and Tony had been doing in the river in the first place. They would want to know what Joel had done to lose his friend that way.

Maybe he could call his dad at work first…before

he went to the police station. His dad would be good at explaining things. His dad would...what would he do? "You're on your honor, Joel." That's what he had said. "You'll be careful the whole way? You won't go anywhere except the park?" And now Joel had proved what his honor was worth, what *he* was worth.

"Come on, kid," the boy said, and though his voice was still rough, it wasn't unkind. He knew. He knew what sort of questions the police would ask, what Joel's father would say, and Joel could tell the boy was feeling sorry for him.

"No," Joel said, shaking his head vigorously and pulling on his shirt. "You go on. I've got my bike here. I'll go report it to the police. No sense you getting involved."

"He's right," the girl said. She held her chin up and spoke with authority, though there were tears running down her cheeks. "There's no sense. Besides, if we go back into town, I might get into trouble. I called in sick to work today, remember? To go with you." She placed an extended index finger in the middle of the boy's chest.

"But it's gotta be reported," the boy said, stubbornly. "And the kid's parents have to be told, too."

At first Joel thought the boy was talking about his

parents, about telling his father and mother, but then he realized the boy meant the Zabrinskys. Joel hadn't thought about Tony's parents up until now. For an instant he imagined ringing the Zabrinskys' doorbell, and he saw Mrs. Zabrinsky, her face tired, her eyes already sad, coming to the door. When the door opened, though, it was Mr. Zabrinsky standing there, a heavy, leather belt in his hand. Joel could feel the cold sweat breaking out along his sides. If the police didn't get him, Tony's father would for sure.

"I'll go to the police," he said. "I promise."

Chapter 7

Joel leaned into his bike, pushing as hard as he could, almost running up the hill. His heart drummed in his ears. The boy and his girl friend were still sitting in their car, probably arguing about whether or not to go to the police. Their presence behind him in the road made the skin between Joel's shoulder blades and up the back of his neck feel tight and bunchy.

When the car finally pulled away, rumbled across the bridge and up the opposite hill, Joel quit pushing and dropped across the handlebars, gasping for breath. After a few moments he looked back. The car was gone. Heat wavered off the empty road.

He began to push his bike again, more slowly now. When he was three fourths of the way to the top, a small red car crested the hill and started toward him. Joel straightened up, freezing his features into what he hoped was an image of innocence, of nonchalance. Still, when the car passed, he had to turn away. If the people in the car got a good look at his face, they would know.

His mother had always told him that he was the worst keeper of guilty secrets in the world. When he was a little kid, if he walked past her with a snitched cookie in his pocket, she would take one look at his face and say, "Joel, what do you have in your pocket?"

Now everybody was going to look at him and say, "Joel, why did you go swimming in the river? Joel, what did you do to your best friend?"

And what kind of questions would the police ask? What would they guess without even asking?

Joel stopped in his tracks, his heart beginning to hammer again. He couldn't go back. He just couldn't!

He jerked his bike around, facing it down the hill and away from town, away from the police, the Zabrinskys, his parents. His climbed on, standing with all his weight on one pedal so that his rear wheel fishtailed as he moved out. This time he would build up enough speed to make it to the top of the other side of the valley without having to get off once to push.

His father had given him permission to ride his bike all the way to Starved Rock State Park. He was going to ride to the park.

A line of fire measured the tops of Joel's thighs. He pedaled steadily, glancing neither to the right nor to the left, images flashing through his brain. The woods at the park were dense. He could hide his bike easily…and then himself. Maybe he could even find a cave in the bluffs that he could stay in. He could live on berries and roots the way the Indians had done. They had hidden out on top of Starved Rock bluff to get away from an enemy tribe, but he couldn't do that. There were footpaths and fences on top of the bluffs now…tourists, too. Anyway, an enemy tribe had trapped the Indians up there, starved them to death, giving the park its name.

A semi roared past, the suction of the huge wheels tugging at Joel and at his bicycle. All he would need to do would be to loosen his grip. The truck would take care of the rest.

Joel stopped pedaling, steered onto the shoulder, and dropped heavily off the bike. What was he doing? Did he really think he was going to hide out? And if he found some place to hide in, how long could he stay? Until he grew up...or died? But it wasn't his fault, was it? Just because he didn't follow his father's orders, that didn't make what happened to Tony his fault.

His father was the one who had said it was all right to ride to the park in the first place. Joel hadn't even wanted to go.

And then there was Tony, crazy Tony, insisting on swimming in the river when he couldn't even swim that well.

Joel expelled a long breath. He felt lighter, somehow. He glanced both ways, then walked his bike across the road and started back in the direction he had come from. He would go home. That was where he belonged...no matter what had happened.

He began to pedal again, his bike in the highest gear so the least movement on his part propelled him the farthest. *Home*, the narrow tires sang against the pavement. *Home.*

There was one thing he needed, though. He needed to decide what to tell his parents—and the Zabrinskys—when they asked about Tony.

He could tell them...he could tell them that he and Tony had started to ride their bikes out to Starved Rock. He could tell them that Tony had stopped when they were crossing the bridge. It was so hot. The river was there... cool and wet. Tony wanted to go swimming.

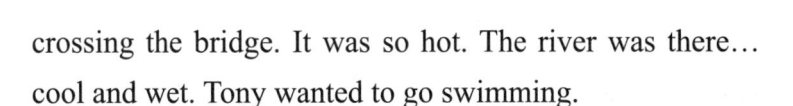

It was the truth, wasn't it?

And then he could tell them how he'd tried to talk Tony out of going into the river. And he could explain that Tony wouldn't listen, because Tony never listened once he had made up his mind. But then Joel would remind his father of the promise he had made that morning. He would say that he told Tony he couldn't go down to the river with him.

He would tell how he had ridden on to Starved Rock by himself. The day was hot, though, and it wasn't much fun riding so far without Tony, so he'd turned around to come back.

The explanation assembled itself in Joel's mind, logical and complete. Why hadn't he thought of it before? What had made him run away? He loosened his clenched fingers, one at a time, from the handlegrips and kept pedaling toward home.

But when he arrived at the top of the ridge overlooking the Vermillion River again, he stopped and stared at the road, the bridge, the wall of trees nearly obscuring the water. If only there were some other way to get home. He didn't know another rout into town, though. Beside, the fire in his thighs had moved into his calves, his shoulders were cramped, and any other route home would undoubtedly be longer than this one.

Joel squeezed the hand brakes and began to creep down the steep hill toward the bridge, the brake pads squealing lightly against the wheels.

Tony had stayed behind to go swimming. That was what Joel would tell everybody. But if he had really ridden on to Starved Rock when Tony had gone down to the water, he would have stopped to check on Tony on the way back…because he wouldn't know.

Joel reached the bridge, still holding the bike in tight control, and pedaled slowly across, keeping his eyes carefully on the road. At the other side, though, he hesitated, stopped, wheeled his bike down the embankment, and propped it against the understructure of the bridge. He would just check…so people wouldn't look at his face when he explained and know he hadn't even checked.

Tony's BMX was still there, carefully obscured in the long grass.

Joel walked slowly toward the riverbank, keeping his mind carefully blank. The whole thing *could* have happened the way he had it figured out. It all made sense.

A squirrel scolded in a nearby tree. The river made a burbling sound, almost as if it were laughing.

There were Tony's clothes scattered haphazardly along the ground, exactly where they had been dropped except for the shirt the girl had moved. One sock hung from a nearby bush; the other lay in the midst of a path of violets.

Sighing over Tony's carelessness, Joel gathered up the clothes, folded them, put them into a neat pile. He folded the pale blue shirt last and laid it on top of the rest, then surveyed the results of his work.

Something was wrong. Tony had never folded his clothes in his life, not unless his mother was standing over him anyway. Joel reached down and mussed the shirt.

As he straightened up, the gleaming surface of the water caught his gaze. The river was unchanged, innocent.

For an instant Joel couldn't breathe. His throat closed, and the air was trapped in his chest in a painful lump. He lifted his hands in surprise, in supplication, but when the breath exploded from him again it brought with it a bleating moan.

Joel stood on the bank clutching at himself and swaying.

Tony was dead…dead.

Chapter 8

"Joel!" The angry voice came immediately after the slammed door. "Joel, where are you?"

Joel lay on his back in the middle of his bed staring at the darkened light fixture. The shadow of the fixture stretched across his ceiling like an elasticized gray spider and bent down the wall. When he had first lain down on the bed, the shadow had been a small blob right next to the light.

"Joel, are you up there?" came his father's voice again, and Joel shook his head slowly from side to side.

No, he wasn't up here. He wasn't anywhere. Hadn't Mrs. Zabrinsky told his father that? All afternoon the telephone had rung at frequent intervals. Then the doorbell. Ding-dong. Ding-dong. Knock, knock, rattle, rattle. First Bobby calling, obviously sent across the street by Mrs.

Zabrinsky, then Mrs. Zabrinsky herself. "Joel! Tony!"

But the house key was in Joel's pocket, and no one could get in...except his parents when they got home from work. They had their own keys. Joel had lain there through the long afternoon and waited for one of them to get home. He had thought it would be his mother who would get there first, though. She usually did get home before his dad because she started work earlier in the morning.

The papers for his route had been dropped on his front porch about two hours before. He had heard the thunk when they hit the concrete, but he hadn't been able to make himself get off the bed to do anything about them. *I could be gone on my route when they come home*, he had thought, but still he hadn't moved.

"Joel!" His door shot open with a report like a firecracker and, as if connected to the door by a spring, he leaped off the bed. The blood rushed from his brain with the sudden movement, and he swayed giddily in the middle of his floor.

"So you *are* here. Mrs. Zabrinsky thought you were."

Joel didn't say anything. He studied a spot on the floor in front of his father's feet.

"What are you doing, locking yourself in the house all

day? What do you mean by this kind of behavior?"

Joel's gaze traveled to his father's belt buckle.

His father was now looking around the room. "Where's Tony?" he asked. "Mrs. Zabrinsky said you two boys spent the entire afternoon locked in the house."

"Tony's not here," Joel said.

"Where is he, then?"

Joel gave a small shrug.

His father ran his fingers through his hair in exasperation. "What's going on, Joel? This isn't like you…sneaking into the house, leaving Tony's mother to worry." He took a step toward Joel, but Joel didn't flinch.

He looked into his father's face, waiting for the blow that he was sure would come…must come. His father had never hit him, but he would now. "I guess I fell asleep," he said. "I didn't hear a thing." He spoke out of the deep calm that had taken hold of him sometime in the long afternoon. "Besides," he added, "it's my house. I can come here if I want to."

Now! His father would hit him now!

Joel's father quit tugging on his hair and dropped his hand. "Of course it's your house," he said quietly, "but you don't have permission to lock yourself in here when

Mrs. Zabrinsky is supposed to be looking after you. She wouldn't have even known you were here if Bobby hadn't caught a glimpse of you going through the door."

"Snoop," Joel said.

"What?" his father asked, beginning to look exasperated again.

"Never mind."

"Well, where is Tony, then? His mother will want to know."

In the river, Joel thought, but out loud he said, "On the road to Starved Rock."

His father tipped his head to one side. He looked skeptical. "Alone?" he asked.

"I came back," Joel said. "Starved Rock was too far, so I came back." Was this what he had planned to say? He wasn't sure.

Bobby appeared in the doorway, his fists cocked on his hips in imitation of their mother's favorite stance when she was cross with either of them. "You guys aren't supposed to be in the house when Mommy and Daddy are gone," he said in his best boy-you're-going-to-get-it voice.

"So what?" Joel snapped back and, instantly deflated, Bobby ducked his head, tucking his thumb into his mouth.

Joel's father was studying his face minutely. "You mean to tell me," he said, "that Tony rode all the way to Starved Rock by himself?"

"I guess he did," Joel said.

"He lied to me, you know, about his mother's giving him permission to go. I found that out from Mrs. Zabrinsky, too."

Joel could feel his father's gaze like a burning pressure. He held his breath, waiting for the moment when all would be known…but his father only shook his head, looked away. "I feel responsible…"

You are responsible, Joel wanted to say. But instead he asked, his voice dull and flat, "Do you want me to go see if I can find him?"

"No, of course not." His father sighed. "It's too far to go back on your bike. Anyway you need to get started on your paper route." He turned and started out of the room, calling back over his shoulder, "I'll telephone the Zabrinskys and tell them that Tony will probably be late."

Very late, Joel thought, and he had a strange urge to laugh. *Tony's dead! Don't you know that?* he wanted to yell. But since it was obvious his father didn't know, that his father didn't know anything, he kicked the leg of his bed and muttered, "Frigging newspapers!"

Bobby's eyes grew round, but his father, though he must have heard, didn't turn back. He wasn't going to *do* anything, no matter what.

"Can I help you with your route today, Joel?" Bobby asked. Bobby was always wanting to help him with his route, with his Scout projects, with anything he did. Sometimes Bobby even helped him when it was his turn on dishes. Dumb little kid.

Joel didn't usually let Bobby go along on his route, though. Tony went along lots of times, but he had his own bike. Balancing Bobby on his bike along with the load of papers was a real trick.

Besides, Tony really helped. He didn't just tag along asking questions and getting in the way.

Tony! Would the Zabrinskys ever find him? The teenager had said something about a body maybe washing up at one of the dams…next week, next month. Maybe. Why hadn't Joel told his father about Tony's going down to the river to swim, about his going on to Starved Rock while Tony went to the river? Then his father could tell the Zabrinskys and the Zabrinskys would know where to look. Somehow nothing had come out right.

"Can I, Joel? Please?" Bobby repeated, and when Joel looked down at his brother, at the eagerness in Bobby's upturned face, his throat closed, and he had to turn away.

"Yeah," he managed to croak, "I guess you can help with my route today."

"Whoowee!" Bobby yelled, and he clapped his pudgy hands and skittered out of the room and back down the stairs.

Joel squared his shoulders and took a deep breath. Then he stopped, breathed again, sniffed. What was that smell in the air? Almost like…almost exactly like dead fish. Joel sniffed his arm, his shirt. That's where it was coming from…him.

Joel drew the neck of his shirt up over his nose and inhaled deeply. There was no question. The stink of the river had followed him home…and his father hadn't noticed that either.

Joel pulled the shirt off, got another from the drawer. The new shirt was fresh—it smelled like his mom's fabric softener—but the light fragrance couldn't cover the stench of the river clinging to his skin.

Joel started down the steps. Maybe nobody knew what a river smelled like.

Bobby was holding the screen door open for their mother. Looking tired and a litter bit frazzled, she set down the grocery bag she was carrying and came to the bottom of the stairs. She stood with her hands on her hips exactly the way Bobby had when he was imitating her earlier. "What on earth were you doing today, Joel? Mrs. Zabrinsky says you and Tony hid in the house all afternoon."

Joel closed his eyes. It was going to start all over again. That was the problem with having two parents. You never heard anything only once. He drew in his breath, composed his face, and continued down the stairs. There was nothing he could do about the smell. "Tony wasn't here," he said, "and I wasn't hiding. I was lying down."

"Lying down?" Joel's mother reached to feel his forehead. "What's the matter? Are you sick?"

"No," Joel answered, submitting to the cool hand pressed to his head, "just not feeling good for a little bit."

"What did you and Tony do today?" his mother asked, her other hand circling the back of his head as though she could feel his temperature better by pressing with both hands. Her eyes were on his face."

"Just rode our bikes."The musky river smell was so strong it made his eyes burn. She had to smell it. There was no way she could miss it.

"How far did you go?"

Joel jerked free, ducking and coming up a few feet down the hall with his back to his mother. "Not very far. Tony was going to ride out to Starved Rock—Dad said we could—but I didn't feel good, like I told you, so I came home."

He couldn't tell what she was doing, behind him as she was, and he didn't want to turn around to look.

"Starved Rock," she repeated. "But that's so far!"

"Dad gave us permission," he said. And then he amended, "He said I could go."

"Well"—a light sigh—"you'd better get busy with your route before people start calling. They'll be complaining about their papers being late."

Joel felt his body go limp. His mother hadn't smelled the river. She hadn't even guessed he was lying. Relief swirled in his brain, curiously mixed with anger. Didn't anybody around here pay attention to anything?

He pushed out the screen door, letting it slam behind him…hard.

Chapter 9

Bobby was squatting on the porch over the stack of newspapers, tugging on the twine that held them, his small, dirty fingers making little headway against the knot.

"You cut it, dummy," Joel said, pulling out his pocket knife. "Like this." He cut the twine on the papers and also on the sack of inserts next to them, his hands moving with angry impatience.

Bobby watched, his lower lip pocking out. "You know I don't got a knife."

"Don't *have*," Joel corrected gruffly, looking away from Bobby's face. "You don't *have* a knife."

"Well, I don't," Bobby said, and he grabbed an advertising circular and stuffed it inside a paper, crumpling both.

"Take it easy," Joel ordered, thumping Bobby on the top of the head with the handle of his knife. "You're going to mess everything up."

Bobby's face rumpled, and he began to cry. "That hurt!" He rubbed the top of his head.

"Everything hurts," Joel mumbled, but now the anger was replaced by shame. What was he on Bobby about? The poor little kid was only trying to help. Joel began pulling the circulars off the stack, one at a time, snapping them into place inside the fold of the papers, rolling the papers to ready them for throwing. *Everything hurts*, he repeated to himself, *except maybe being dead. Being dead's probably the only thing that's easy.*

The thought made his skin go cold and tingly.

"What's wrong, Joel?" Bobby asked. "Why do you look like that?" His own pain forgotten, Bobby was staring with enormous green eyes.

"Nothing," Joel said, but the word came out sounding squeezed. "If you're going to help, start putting the papers in the bag."

Bobby began bagging the papers, but he didn't take his eyes off Joel's face.

"Watch what you're doing," Joel snapped, pulling the anger around himself again like a cloak. "We've gotta get this show on the road."

Bobby nodded sharply and set to loading the rolled papers into the bag as fast as Joel could get them ready.

Joel stuffed and rolled, the fury taking over again, but this time he knew whom he wanted to punch. It was all Tony's fault. All of it! Tony knew what a poor swimmer he was. He had to have realized the risks. And now he had gone off and left Joel to answer for him. And what was he going to say?

Tony's parents would probably be asking questions by the time he got home from his route. *Tony isn't home, Joel. Where could he be? You're the last one who saw him...alive.*

"Damn it all, anyway!" Joel cried, pushing the rest of the stack of papers off the porch. "I'm sick of this stinking paper route."

Bobby was sitting back on his heels, his eyes in danger of swallowing up his face. He peered over the edge of the porch and then up at Joel. "You squashed three of Mommy's purple things," he said.

Joel looked, too. The papers were lying in the middle of his mother's petunia bed.

"Do you want me to get the papers back?" Bobby asked. "I think if we brush them off they'll still be okay."

"All right," Joel consented. "Get them back."

Bobby climbed down the steps and then up again. He peered cautiously over the stack of papers he carried. "They're okay, Joel," he said, laying them down reverently, as though they were jewels.

Joel shook his head, trying to dispel the red fog that had taken possession of his brain. If he could get his hands on Tony now, he would…But that was ridiculous. What would he do? What could anybody do? Beat Tony up?

At the thought he let out a choking guffaw, half laughter, half sob.

Bobby was watching him again, his face wary, his lower lip clenched between small, white teeth. "Are you okay, Joel?" he asked.

"Yeah," Joel said. "I'm okay." He went back to preparing the papers. "I'm alive, aren't I?"

The paper route seemed endless. Bobby rode behind Joel on the bicycle seat and chattered the whole way. Joel tried to listen, with half an ear anyway, but he couldn't. With each thunk of a paper on porch, he heard, instead, Tony's voice, challenging, teasing. "I'll bet you can't get one in the middle of Mrs. McCullough's hanging geraniums. I'll bet you can't clip the Smiths' cat. Why don't you...?"

Joel wanted to yell at Tony, to tell him to shut up, but even Bobby would think he was crazy if he started yelling at a voice inside his own head.

Why did he feel so *responsible*, as though he had pushed Tony in? Why did he always have to feel responsible for *everything* that happened? If they had gone climbing on the bluffs and he, Joel, had fallen, Tony wouldn't have blamed himself. Would he?

Tony had said once that Joel was like an old grandmother, fretting all the time. Well, Tony ought to see him now. He would laugh.

At the thought of Tony laughing, Joel almost smiled. He and Tony always had so much fun together. Besides the tree house they were building this summer, they had a lot of other projects going. They always did.

For one thing, they had been pooling their allowances to buy a worm farm. Their plan was to get rich selling bait. Tony had even had the idea of using his mother's meat grinder to grind whatever worms were left at the end of the summer and sell them as goldfish food. (That was because Joel's father had pointed out that neither family would want worms multiplying in the basement over the winter.)

For his part, Joel was skeptical about whether there were very many people anxious to buy worm mash for goldfish food, but he hadn't said that to Tony.

Last summer they had concocted a wonderful scheme for getting rich selling decorative pennies. They flattened fifty pennies by leaving them on the tracks to be run over by the 3:45 train, turning them into thin, coppery disks. Their plan hadn't been exactly what anybody could call successful, though. They sold only one penny, because every other kid in town knew how to flatten pennies, too. The one they sold (for a nickel) was to a prissy girl whose mother wouldn't allow her to go near the tracks. They had been left with forty-nine pennies they couldn't spend, not even in a gumball machine.

Joel tossed the last paper and turned his bike toward home. Bobby had finally fallen silent, and Joel was grateful for that. He could feel his brother's small, hot hands gripping his shirt and the puffs of breath on the back of his neck, so close, so alive.

A surge of protectiveness passed through Joel. He would have to teach Bobby how to swim. Bobby was afraid even to get his face in the water. Joel would start working with him right away. Every kid needed to know how to swim. Sometimes parents didn't seem to realize what a dangerous place the world is.

When Joel turned the corner by his house, he could see his mother and father in the front yard, talking to Mr. and Mrs. Zabrinsky. Seeing the four of them standing there, their faces solemn and intent, sent a chill through Joel's bones. What were they talking about? What did they know? By now, someone must have seen through his lie.

Or maybe the teenage boy had come back and turned Joel in.

Joel coasted up the driveway and stepped off his bike, pushing it into the garage before Bobby had a chance to climb down. Inside the garage, he scooped Bobby off the seat and set him on the floor.

"Thanks, bubby," he said. "I appreciate your help." He propped his bike along the wall, out of the way of the cars.

"I'll help you again tomorrow, Joel," Bobby said, his face glowing in the semidarkness of the garbage.

"We'll see," Joel said, patting Bobby's shoulder. He began tinkering with his bicycle, shifting the gears back and forth uselessly, pretending to be engrossed.

Bobby watched him for a moment, then turned and headed outside with a one-legged skip. "Mommy, Daddy," he called before he was even beyond the front of the garage. "Joel's gonna let me help him with his paper route tomorrow, too."

Joel stood where he was, trying to control the way his hands trembled, the way the muscles in his face seemed to jerk. They were talking about *him* out there. He was certain of it. But there was no way past them without being seen, and if he stayed in the garage any longer, they would probably notice that, too. He shifted the gears one last time, slumped his shoulders, and pulled his head in, like a turtle retreating into its shell. Then he stepped out into the staring light of the driveway.

Chapter 10

"Joel, would you come here for a moment, please?" Joel's father called.

Joel hesitated, wondering if he dared pretend he hadn't heard, but then he turned slowly and, keeping his head down, moved in the direction of his father's voice.

"The Zabrinskys want to know where you saw Tony last," his father said when he had arrived at his side.

Joel had a sudden image of Tony laughing, the river water streaming from his dark hair. "On the road," he said. "On the road to Starved Rock."

"But where on the road?" Mr. Zabrinsky asked. "How far had you boys gone before you turned back?" Mr. Zabrinsky was a big man, with huge, rather hairy hands. He sounded impatient.

"Oh," Joel said, scuffing the head off of a dandelion

with the toe of his sneaker, "about as far as the bridge over the river, I guess."

"The bridge over the river!" Mrs. Zabrinsky repeated with a small gasp.

Mr. Zabrinsky leaned toward Joel. "But he was on his way to Starved Rock. Right?"

"Right," Joel mumbled, wishing, again, that he had remembered the first time to tell the story he had originally planned.

"Besides," Mrs. Zabrinsky said, "Tony can't swim. He'd know better than to go near the river." She seemed to be trying to reassure herself.

"He can't swim?" Joel asked, squinting up at her. "Really?"

She smiled, a crooked half smile that Joel had seen a million times. "You must know that, Joel. You've gone to the pool with him…when he's willing to go."

Joel shrugged, tried to look away. "Well, he mostly played on the slide—or on the ropes, you know?—but he never told me he couldn't swim."

Mrs. Zabrinsky touched Joel's arm, and without thinking he jerked away. His skin felt clammy, and he was sure the stink of the river rose from him like a vapor.

"Maybe I shouldn't have told you," she said. "Maybe he wouldn't want you to know. He tried swimming lessons once, but he was always afraid of the water."

Tony? Afraid? Joel pushed the thought away.

"Is that all?" he asked, stuffing his hands into his pockets.

"Yes," his father said. "I guess that's all." And as Joel walked away, trying to look casual, trying to remember how his feet used to move when he wasn't thinking about them, his father added to the Zabrinskys, "Let's call the park ranger. If he doesn't know anything, then we should probably drive out there, take a look for ourselves."

"I suppose I shouldn't worry," Mrs. Zabrinsky replied, "but you know what Tony's like. I guess I worry more about him than all the rest of the kids rolled up together."

Joel stepped through the front door into the cool darkness of the hall. Why hadn't Tony thought about his mother, about the way she worried, before he had decided to go for a swim?

Joel stood in the shower, the water streaming over his skin. He had soaped three times, his hair, everything, and rinsed and soaped again. The water was beginning to grow cool, so he would have to get out soon. His mother would be cross with him for using all the hot water.

He turned off the shower, toweled dry. As he rubbed his skin, the smell rose in his nostrils again, the dead-fish smell of the river.

He considered getting back into the shower, but he didn't. It wouldn't help. He knew that.

He pulled on his pajama bottoms and walked through the dark hall to his bedroom. Bobby was in bed, probably already asleep. Lights were on downstairs, and the murmur of his parents' voices floated up the stairwell. They were talking about Tony, of course. What else?

He didn't turn on a light in his room. He simply headed for the dark shape of his bed and lay down on top of the spread, arranging his arms and legs gingerly, as if they pained him.

After a while he heard light footsteps on the stairs, and then his mother came into his room. She sat down next to him on the bed, so close that he knew she had to be pretending not to be offended by the smell.

"Joel," she said, "are you sure you've told us everything you know?"

"About what?" he demanded roughly, as if he didn't

understand what she meant, wishing it were possible not to understand.

"About Tony, about what you boys did today."

For an instant he thought about telling her. It would have been such a relief to let the words spill out, to let the choking tears come. But then he thought about having to tell the Zabrinskys, too, and the police, and about the twisted disappointment in his father's face, and he couldn't. He simply couldn't. He flopped over onto his stomach, muffling his response with the pillow.

"I already told you…I got tired and came home. I don't know what Tony did."

"Did you boys have a fight?" she asked gently.

Joel remembered being mad at Tony, but he couldn't remember, now, why he'd been mad. Especially he remembered saying, "You're the one who's scared."

"No," he said. "We didn't have a fight."

His mother continued to sit there, as though she expected him to say more, and after a while Joel began to hold his tongue tightly between his teeth. It was the only way he knew to hang on to the words that threatened to come tumbling out of his mouth. *I know where Tony is*, he wanted to say. *I can tell you exactly where to begin looking.*

Finally his mother leaned over and kissed the back of his head, then got up to go. After she had left the room, Joel unlocked his jaws, relishing the burning pain in his tongue.

A few minutes later he heard his father's footsteps on the stairs, heard him stop just outside his room. He waited there for a long time, but Joel pretended to be asleep, lying perfectly still and concentrating on keeping his breathing steady and slow. Finally his father went away, too.

Joel buried his face in his pillow, pressing his nose and mouth into the suffocating darkness. It would have been better if he and Tony had tied themselves together and climbed the bluffs. At least he wouldn't have been left behind.

Chapter 11

Joel lay waiting. He stared into the darkness until his eyes ached, straining to see, to hear, though he didn't know what he was waiting for.

When he heard a sound at last, the soft swish of automobile tires on pavement, the hollow thud of doors closing, muted voices, he stood and moved quickly to his window.

A car had stopped in front of the Zabrinskys' house, and two men were walking up to their front door.

Joel gasped. Police! The men were police officers! The teenage boy must have reported him after all!

He tried to pull his jeans on over his pajamas, but his foot got tangled in the fabric. He kicked the jeans out of his way and hurtled down the stairs. He had to explain! If the police found out from Mr. and Mrs. Zabrinsky about the lie he had told...

The front door was locked, and he lost precious seconds fiddling with it, jerking the lock this way and that until the door finally sprang toward him and he pushed the screen door out of his way. But at the edge of the porch, he stopped, caught his balance on the top step.

Across the street, Mr. Zabrinsky stood silhouetted in his front doorway, talking to the officers. Behind him, Tony's mother moved through the lighted hall toward the front door and the cluster of men. Joel's stomach twisted. He was too late.

He turned to go back inside, but the door opened and his father stepped onto the porch, buttoning a short-sleeved shirt. Joel looked to see if his mother was coming, too, but she wasn't. She must already have gone to sleep.

"Come on, son," his father said. "Let's see if there's anything we can do."

No! Joel wanted to whisper, to shout. *I'm not going over there.* Not a single sound came out of his mouth, though, and when his father put a hand on his shoulder, he seemed to lose all capacity to resist. He turned and walked with his father toward the Zabrinskys' house.

"Here's the boy who was with Tony," Mr. Zabrinsky

was saying as Joel and his father joined the officers on the porch. Mr. Zabrinsky spoke without inflection. All the life seemed to have been squeezed out of his voice.

The two policemen pivoted simultaneously to face Joel, their eyes shadowed by the visors of their caps, their mouths set lines. One of them held a plastic bag from which he had drawn Tony's pale blue shirt. Joel stepped backward, but his father held an arm behind him. Joel couldn't tell if his father was protecting him or preventing him from running away.

"What have you found?" his father asked.

"The boy's clothes," the officer holding the shirt said. "By the river. His bike, too."

Joel stole a glimpse at Tony's mother. She was swaying, her hands pressed against her face. Did she know the truth? Did she know he had been there, that he had seen it all? He couldn't tell.

"Did you know Tony went down to the river, Joel?" Mr. Zabrinsky asked in the same lifeless voice he had used at first.

"No," Joel said. "I didn't know anything. I got tired, like I told you. I…" They were all looking at him, the police officers, Tony's parents, his father. Staring. Again Joel started to back away, and again his father's arm prevented him from doing so. The slight pressure of the arm along his back made him want to strike out, to break away and run. If he could get away, he could hide someplace where those terrible eyes couldn't follow. Why had he come back from Starved Rock? He couldn't seem to remember.

"Okay," he said. "Okay. Tony said he was going to go swimming. I tried to stop him. I told him the river was dangerous."

"And did you see him go into the water?" one of the officers asked, stepping closer to Joel.

The other one moved in closer, too, asking, "Were you there?"

"No!" Joel cried. "No!"

"Nobody's blaming you, son," the first officer said. "But the more you can tell your friend's parents"—he indicated the Zabrinskys with one hand as though directing Joel's attention to a picture or a statue in the doorway there—"the easier it will be. It's the not-knowing that's the worst."

"Please," Mrs. Zabrinsky whispered. "If you know anything…"

Mr. Zabrinsky leaned against the doorframe, one

massive fist pressed tightly against his mouth, weeping silently.

"Joel?" his father said. "You've got to tell us." And then he turned to the others and added, laying his arm heavily across Joel's shoulders, "Joel is an honorable boy. He'll tell you what he knows."

Honorable! Joel staggered beneath the weight of his father's arm, then pulled away, teetering on the edge of the porch. The five faces bent toward him were like five pale moons, but it was his father's face that loomed the largest.

He took a deep breath. "Tony wanted to climb the bluffs at Starved Rock, and I was scared to do it. So when he changed his mind, when he decided to go swimming instead...I thought...I thought..." He was shaking all over as he spoke. "I looked for him. When he went under, I tried to find him. But I couldn't....He just...he just...disappeared."

"Oh...Joel!" The arm that had been holding him didn't reach out to touch him again. "Joel!" his father repeated.

Mr. Zabrinsky moaned and stepped backward into the shadowy hall. Tony's mother stood perfectly still. She didn't look at her husband. She stared only at Joel, her face twisted and ugly.

Everybody was looking at him, blaming him. He wanted to turn away, to run at last, but his feet refused to carry him in that direction. Instead, he stumbled toward his father, his hands raised and clenched into fists. "I hate you!" he cried, pounding at his father's chest. "It's all your fault. You never should have let me go!"

His father said nothing, did nothing to shield himself from Joel's fists. He simply stood there, absorbing the force of the blows until Joel could bear it no longer. He turned and leaped off the porch and bolted across the street.

But even as he slammed through the door and ran up the stairs to his room, he knew. It wasn't his father he hated. It wasn't his father at all.

He was the one...Tony had died because of him.

Chapter 12

Joel lay curled on his side, facing his bedroom door. That's where his father would appear when he came to punish him. He would have to do it this time. He wouldn't have any choice.

He would punish him for yelling at him...for hitting him...for daring Tony to swim out to the sandbar.

Joel had known from the beginning that it was his fault. From the moment Tony had disappeared, he had understood. Running away hadn't changed a thing, and coming back hadn't changed anything either.

Nothing could change what had happened...ever.

A light summer breeze fanned across the bed, rustled the leaves on the maple tree outside his window. It was the tree Joel and Tony had been building a tree house in. The sound of leaves, the touch of cool air on his skin, was good. It was good to be able to feel such things, but Tony couldn't. Tony couldn't feel anything anymore.

Joel lifted his arm to his nose and sniffed. The smell was still there, so sharp that it made his eyes sting. He supposed it would be with him for the rest of his life.

Why had he been dumb enough to dare Tony, anyway? He knew what Tony was like. If somebody had dared him to walk through fire, he would have done that, too.

Joel pulled the pillow over his head, pushed it off again. His eyes were as dry and scratchy as sandpaper. He wished his father would come, get it over with.

The front door opened and closed again. Joel could hear his father fiddling with the lock. Didn't he understand yet? Bad wasn't something that could be locked out. Bad was something that came from inside you when you didn't even know it was there.

His father was moving up the stairs now, his footsteps heavy and slow, and he stopped outside Joel's door as he had earlier in the evening. Joel lay quietly, holding his muscles rigid, although he knew pretending to be asleep wouldn't work this time.

His father came in. He pulled a chair away from Joel's desk, set it next to the bed, very close, and sat down. At first he didn't say anything, and Joel thought, *He's going to sit there all night. That's his way to punish me. He's going to sit there so I can't run away, so I can't sleep, so I couldn't even cry if I wanted to.*

Joel tried to keep his breathing steady and slow the way he had done before, but he felt as though he had been running for a long time and had to gasp for air. His skin was too tight. He was going to explode.

"I'm sorry," his father said finally.

"Sorry?" Joel blurted, astonishment rolling him over onto his back. "Why are *you* sorry?"

His father didn't answer at first, and just when Joel was convinced he wasn't ever going to answer, he said, "I'm sorry I misjudged the situation. I'm sorry I gave you permission to go."

Joel didn't respond.

"And," his father added softly, "I'm sorry that I wasn't there to help you, that you had to be so frightened and so alone."

"It was my fault," Joel said dully. "The whole thing was my fault."

"Probably nobody could have found Tony in that water," his father replied, not understanding. "And if you had managed somehow, he might have pulled you under. He was bigger than you, heavier. He wouldn't have known what he was doing."

Joel thought of the swirling water closing over his head, pouring into his lungs, and his skin rippled into gooseflesh. But then he thought of Tony, Tony taking dibs on *his* bike, Tony dancing a jig on the bridge, Tony pretending to be a prehistoric monster. "It should have been me," he said.

Joel's father took hold of his arm, almost roughly. "Don't you say that," he said. "Don't you ever let me hear you say that."

Joel looked his father full in the face. "It's my fault," he repeated. "If I hadn't gone down to the river, Tony would have stayed out of the water."

"Maybe," his father said. "Maybe not. There's no way to know. You can't liver your life by *maybes*."

Joel's arm was beginning to hurt where his father gripped it, but that wasn't enough. Nothing his father said or did was enough. "Are you going to punish me?" he asked.

His father sighed, was silent again for a moment, his hand gently smoothing away the earlier pressure. "Is that what you want?"

"You said I was on my honor this morning. I wasn't supposed to go anywhere except the park."

His father merely asked, "What would it teach you, son...more punishment?"

Since Joel had no answer for that, he said the only thing he could think of to say, said it harshly, as though it were an accusation. "Your hand is going to smell like it."

"Like what?" His father raised his hand to his face.

"Like the river. Don't you notice the stink?"

His father sniffed his hand again, bent over to bring his nose close to Joel's skin, then straightened. "I don't know what you mean, Joel. I can't smell anything."

"But *I* can smell it," Joel wailed. "It won't go away."

His father didn't say anything.

"Make it go away," Joel spoke in a whisper, as if they were discussing another person standing in the room, someone who could be forced to leave.

His father smoothed the hair back from Joel's face. "I can't," he said, very quietly.

The anger surged through Joel's veins. He wanted to push his father away, to pummel him again. What good was this man who couldn't protect him from bad things happening and wouldn't punish him to make things right? "You don't understand," he said through clenched teeth. "I dared Tony to swim out to the sandbar. I knew he couldn't swim all that well. I must have known. And I dared him."

Joel expected…he didn't know what he expected, actually. Maybe he expected the world to fall in. At the very least he expected his father to rise up in rage. Instead there followed only another silence, the kind that made him want to scream. He held himself carefully rigid, though, and didn't move, only waited.

"It's going to be a hard thing to live with, for both of us," his father said at last. "But there is nothing else to be done."

Joel sat up. He was shouting now. "What are you talking about…we? *You* didn't do anything. You didn't even know you shouldn't have let me go!"

"But we all made choices today, Joel. You, me, Tony. Tony's the only one who doesn't have to live with his choice."

For a moment Joel could only stare, uncomprehending, at this man who wouldn't…couldn't take away his pain. Tony was free, while he, he and his father, would have to live with this terrible day forever. And though Joel clenched his jaw and squeezed his eyes shut, it was no use. He began to sob.

"Ah," his father said, as if relieved, and he leaned forward, drawing Joel onto his lap. Joel felt awkward, oversized. Surely there was no longer room for him here. But his father wrapped his arms around him tightly, and Joel's cheek settled into the hollow between his chest and shoulder. The racking sobs flowed out of him like water.

His father held him for a long time, saying nothing, until Joel's tears came without sound and his breaths were quivering gasps. Even then, his father held him. After a while, Joel began to pattern his breathing to match the steady rising and falling of his father's chest.

"I'd like to go back to bed now," he said finally. His father, instead of simply releasing him, reached forward to strip back the covers, then stood and laid him gently in the bed. He pulled the sheet up and tucked it beneath Joel's chin.

He will leave me now, Joel thought, but his father sat down in the chair once more.

Joel turned on his side, facing his father this time. He was tired, exhausted, but tinglingly awake. He was also empty, as though he had been hollowed out with a knife. He tried to think of something to say, if only to hear his father's voice.

"Do you believe in heaven?" he asked at last. "Do you believe Tony's gone there?"

His father bent toward him. "If there is a heaven, I'm sure Tony's gone there," he replied. "I can't imagine a heaven that could be closed to charming, reckless boys."

If! Joel felt as if he were sinking through the bed. "What do you mean…*if* there's a heaven?"

"I don't suppose anybody knows," his father answered gently, "what happens after." He hesitated, and one hand came up, described a series of circles in the air, then settled into his lap again as though it had finished the statement for him. "I believe there's something about life that goes on. It seems too good to end in a river."

Joel let his father's words sift through him slowly. He had hoped for something firmer, more certain. *Yes, there is a heaven. Certainly Tony is there now.* He would have to settle, though, for what he got.

And what he got was a gentle summer night, a hollow place inside his gut that felt as though it might never be filled, and this man, his dad, who sat beside his bed.

"Will you stay?" he asked, reaching a hand out tentatively to touch his father's knee. "Will you sit with me until I fall asleep?"

"Of course," his father said.

名·家·书·评

人格能担保什么？

儿童文学评论家　张子樟

一

哪些是孩子成长过程中应培养的美德？20世纪90年代初，美国里根时代的教育部长本内特（William J. Bennett）发现，当代家长在教育孩子时方式有些偏差。因为只重视孩子未来的成就，所以教养重心几乎全放在教导孩子如何在学业、运动场上或职场上跟他人竞争，把孩子的成就放在一切之上，不管（或忽略）他们的礼仪与品德。在他看来，家长只教育孩子追求个人利益，而忽略品德教育，会使孩子未来必然处在一个更不安全、更不幸福的社会环境中。身为教育家，他特别重视品德教育，于是开始从世界经典名著中搜集能对读者产生励志作用、展现和培养珍贵恒久的美德的故事，编著了《美德书》（The Book of Virtues: A Treasury of Great Moral Stories）。全书分为十大主题：自律、怜悯、责任、友谊、工作、勇气、毅力、诚实、忠诚、信仰。

由于这本书过于厚重，出版社便请本内特将其筛选成适合儿童阅读或聆听的三十一篇文字，成为《孩子的美德书》（The Children's Book of Virtues），原来的十大主题也变成勇气和毅力，责任、工作和自律，怜悯和信仰，诚实、忠诚和友谊四大类。

台湾大学精神科医生宋维村先生在为《汉声精选世界成长文学》系列撰写的序文中提到了少年人格成长的十大必备品德：勇

气、正义、爱心、道德、伦理、友谊、自律、奋斗、责任、合作。对照之下，他的说法与本内特的重叠颇多，这点足以证明中外学者都想借文学作品作为品德教育的辅助工具，在潜移默化中，提升读者的品格。纽伯瑞获奖作品中有许多涉及上述的品德主题，1987年银牌奖作品——玛丽昂·戴恩·鲍尔（Marion Dane Bauer）的《出事的那一天》（On My Honor），便是一个极佳的例子。

二

读《出事的那一天》很容易让人想起《通往特拉比西亚的桥》（Bridge to Terabithia）。这两本书都谈到友谊与死亡，书中好友的突然过世，使得主角需要长期自我调适，才能重新生活。不同的是，《通往特拉比西亚的桥》中女主角之死，纯粹是意外；《出事的那一天》里汤尼之死，好友乔是间接杀害者，终其一生，乔都得背负这一永恒的内疚。

两个主角都是十二岁。汤尼个性鲁莽，容易冲动，我行我素，不愿受人约束，从来不理会别人对他的看法。乔比较内向，做事欠缺果断，总是犹豫再三，或希望他人承担部分责任。两个人个性差很多，却硬凑在一起。汤尼找到一个可以衬托并突显自己好冒险的精神伙伴；乔却想仰赖汤尼，从无趣生活中找到一些好玩之事，两个人竟因此成为好友。

乔在汤尼的激将之下，要求他父亲答应他与汤尼骑自行车去饿死岩，他确信父亲不会答应。没想到乔的父亲竟勉强点头，但要乔以人格保证，除了公园之外，不会到别的地方。一路上，两人一直在比赛骑车技术和力气。到了威米兰河时，汤尼一时兴起，坚持下河游泳。乔起初不肯，因为这条河非常危险，但禁不起汤尼的言语刺激，所以也跟着下水。两人在水中依然互相嘲弄对方。乔在气愤之下，要汤尼一起游到沙洲，汤尼根本不识水性，在途中溺水。乔虽回头在水中找他，并在公路上拦截一个青年，向他求救，依然找不到汤尼。

三

事情发生后，剩余的故事全部是仔细述说乔如何处理汤尼的死亡。他没有照着大人要求他做的来做。他的反应十分可信与适当。汤尼的死亡对乔造成重大的打击。一直到接近故事结束时，责任感才压倒似的得以实现。这件事会跟随他一辈子。在以后的日子里，乔内心深处依旧要遭受无穷无尽的煎熬与折磨。

读者关切的是故事的另一半重心，即乔在面临此次突发事件时如何设法处理。也就是说，能否适当刻画出乔自我挣扎的心路历程，是对作者功力的验证。这本书最令人称赞的就是这部分。作者以细腻的手法，详实地描绘了乔的懊恼、后悔、逃避、说谎、焦躁、无助、绝望、崩溃、指认等的经过。乔同时也回忆从前与汤尼一起时的美好日子。他一再拖延，但警察出现时，他只得面对现实，说出实话，并归罪于父亲："都是你的错！你根本不应该让我们去的。"实际上，他恨的是他自己，因为汤尼是因他而死。名誉保证、人格保证全无意义。

四

这是一本关于同侪压力、谎言和罪恶的书。简单说来，它涉及了青春期的罪与死。这篇故事并非个案，它具有普遍性，因为在现实生活中，我们可找到无数的汤尼与乔。他们往往因一时的冲动或不理智而造成无法挽救的后果。这个阶段的孩子说大不大，说小不小。他们认为自己够大了，想要独立面对自己的挑战，不想让大人干预；但有时又认为自己太小，需要成人的庇佑与一再呵护。

一些青少年认为，这世上没有一件事是不可克服的，相信不会有不幸的事发生在他们身上，所以飙车、吸毒、酗酒、不顾后果，不停地糟蹋自己，毫不珍惜美好的青春年华。固然情绪不稳定、冒险与叛逆是青少年的部分特征，但在成长过程中也需同时养成勇气、诚实、自律、责任等品德。或许这本书可提醒读者：凡事必三思。

作者玛丽昂·戴恩·鲍尔充分掌握了青少年的心理变化过程，角色刻画与对白自然，把乔和汤尼的性格诠释得十分透彻，并深刻地描绘出一个十二岁的孩子面临的两难状况。主题会给一些孩子不舒服的感觉（大人显然也不例外）。但不幸的是，同侪压力是人生中必须面对的一件大事。在成长过程中，每个孩子都必然会有一些同侪压力的经历。对乔这个悲伤男孩良心不安的过程的写实刻画容易引发读者对父子两人的同情。随着情节推进，事件逐渐明朗，读者会深感愤怒、恐惧及惋惜。同时，另一个阅读角度也不应忽略。很多孩子都认为自己永远不会死，因此他们一无所惧。但身为父母的人对此一清二楚，他们想尽办法来帮助自己的子女，让其健康成长，度过心灵和生活的难关。这本书讨论的就是孩子成长中这种一无所惧的态度，以及事情有变得不可收拾的可能性。

作者介绍

认识玛丽昂·戴恩·鲍尔

提起玛丽昂·戴恩·鲍尔(Marion Dane Bauer)，美国人都知道她是位有名的作家，获得过许多奖项。其作品从学龄前儿童看的短诗、图画书，到适合青少年阅读的小说、写作指导，到成人读物，无所不包。她还为老师和图书馆儿童期刊编写故事和撰写文章。然而她的成就不止于此。在美国文学圈中，玛丽昂·戴恩·鲍尔更被人视为优秀的导师，她不断提升儿童文学的写作艺术，并且毫不吝啬地与后进分享自己的所知。某位作家就曾说：如果不是鲍尔的支持，他的作品"到现在还在废纸堆里"。鲍尔在文坛受人敬重的程度，由此可以想见。

1938年，鲍尔出生在美国伊利诺伊州奥格尔斯比小镇，在那里度过了童年，后来她用"田园风光"来形容她的家乡。她先后就读于伊利诺伊州社区大学和密苏里州立大学。大学时，鲍尔原本主修新闻摄影，大二转攻英文，从此以此为业。鲍尔写的第一首诗是为了纪念她的泰迪熊。她写了很多故事。兴趣引导她成为一名英语老师。但是她成为职业作家是在她的女儿上小学的时候,从此她笔耕不辍。鲍尔的作品中,《出事的那一天》(On My Honor)曾获得1987年的纽伯瑞银牌奖,是其中最受欢迎的作品,至今许多学校仍采用这本书作为阅读教材。另外,《你的故事什么样》(What's Your Story)是一本谈论写作的书,曾获得美国图书馆协会的好书奖。其他较为著名的作品还包括:《信任问题》(A Question of Trust)、《像妈妈又像女儿》(Like Mother like Daughter)、《我忧愁吗?》(Am I Blue)等等。

《出事的那一天》里的整个故事真实地发生在鲍尔的童年。她十三岁的时候和一个叫拉尔夫的好朋友,还有另一个不知道名字的男孩一起去威米兰河游泳。那条河很浑浊、很危险，禁止游泳。可是由于某种原因——鲍尔不知道是什么原因，或许是天太热而河水很凉——拉尔夫和那个男孩下了水。实际上他们只是在河里趟着走。可是，那个男孩不会游泳，突然跌进水里，越陷越深……再也没有出来。拉尔夫反复潜进水中寻找，可是都没有找到。直到拉尔夫最后从水中出来的时候，他才意识到自己的朋友已经被淹死了。他感到非常害怕和内疚，知道自己做了不该做的事情。他回到家，冲进自己的房间，关上门，没有和任何人说发生了什么。

后来，拉尔夫和鲍尔一直是非常好的朋友，但是他再也没提起这件事，他非常不喜欢和别人谈论这件事。很多年以后鲍尔给孩子们写故事的时候，她想起了这件事，把它作为一个故事基础，再一次重现了当时她和朋友面对此事的感受。

鲍尔说，从某种意义上，她根据真事创作了《出事的那一天》。但她不希望这是一个关于拉尔夫的故事，她希望创作的角色不是拉尔夫，涉及的家庭也不是拉尔夫的家庭。拉尔夫没有告诉鲍尔他对整个事件的感受，在书中乔的想法和感受是以鲍尔曾经有过的经历写成的。她在小时候做了羞愧的事情后，总是尽力去忘掉，自己去找解决的办法。她不知道拉尔夫是否有爸爸的呵护。但她在书里写成了乔和爸爸一起面对这件事情，于是这个故事就产生了。事实上，鲍尔的其他故事也是这么产生的。它可能来自报纸上的一篇文章、在杂货店里偶然听到的或是某个朋友说的一件事。但是，创作中一定渗入了鲍尔自己的想法和感受。

除了写作，教学一直是鲍尔终身热爱的工作。也因为如此，她不断将自己的写作经验与心得化成美好的文字，传授给任何有心于写作的人。即使退休以后，她的家里仍然长期维持每周一次的写作班，而且各地的学生（不必一定是她教过的）也都可以组队前往拜访，与她聊聊写作的话题，或请她接受采访。

认识鲍尔的人对她热爱生活的积极态度无不留下深刻印象。她非常有活力，喜欢露营、登山和尝试各种新鲜事物，并用心去体会。她自认为强烈的感受力就是她写作的灵感来源。

1.《惠灵顿传奇》

著者：[美]艾伦·阿姆斯特朗/绘者：S．D．申德勒/译者：余国芳

　　2006年纽伯瑞银牌奖。在一间挤满了"遗弃动物"的谷仓里，有退休的赛马、过度亢奋的公鸡、一群又矮又吵的母鸡、一只名叫大小姐的莫斯科鸭子以及新来的神秘大猫惠灵顿，还有时常来造访的狗、老鼠和一对学习吃力的小姐弟。大猫惠灵顿用分段式的方法，讲述了一个令大家既惊叹又感动的冒险故事——他的祖先和一位少年狄克·惠灵顿互相支持、发迹致富的传奇经历。

2.《少女苏菲的航海故事》

著者：[美]沙伦·克里奇/译者：王玲月

　　2001年纽伯瑞银牌奖。苏菲从小父母双亡，却表现得似乎没有这回事；苏菲是个怕水的女孩，却坚持要参加跨海之旅；苏菲心中埋藏着深深的恐惧和忧伤，在航行中却表现得十分坚强，事事都要自己完成……一次神奇惊险的家族跨海之旅，驱散了苏菲内心深处的阴影，让她摆脱了自幼丧亲的不安和悲痛，让她勇敢地面对现实，让她得到自信与成长。

3.《我叫巴德，不叫巴弟》

著者：[美]克里斯托弗·保罗·柯蒂斯/译者：甄晏

　　2000年纽伯瑞金牌奖。巴德很小就失去了母亲，也从来没有见过父亲。寄养家庭的生活让他不能忍受，他决定出逃去找他的父亲。母亲从来没有告诉过他父亲是谁，但他认为母亲留下的传单中有线索，一定可以让他找到自己的亲生父亲。什么也阻止不了他，不管是困难、饥饿、恐惧还是"吸血鬼"……小小的巴德历经挫折，最后终于找到了关爱他、呵护他的亲人。

4.《印第安人的麂皮靴》

著者：[美]沙伦·克里奇/译者：王玲月

　　1995年纽伯瑞金牌奖。少女莎儿的好友菲比一家接连收到怪异的信件。接着出现一位指名要找菲比母亲的神秘男子，没多久菲比的母亲离奇失踪……莎儿也经历过母亲不告而别的痛苦和困惑，她决定帮助菲比找到母亲。莎儿在帮助朋友的过程中悟出了很多道理，她和爷爷奶奶一起踏上了旅程，追寻母亲的脚步，穿上了母亲的"麂皮靴"，明白了母亲出走的真正原因。

5.《数星星》

著者：[美]洛伊丝·劳里/**译者：**汴桥

1990年纽伯瑞金牌奖。什么叫勇敢？这个问题让年仅十岁的安妮在心中想了又想，但总是弄不明白。自从纳粹占领丹麦之后，安妮小时候熟悉的很多事物就从生活中消失了。每个街道转角总是有站岗的德国士兵……直到纳粹在丹麦展开追捕犹太人的行动，当安妮必须挺身而出保护她的犹太朋友时，她才第一次通过自己的摸索与表现，深深体会了保持勇气的艰难……《数星星》不论从文学、历史还是励志的角度来说，都是一本值得任何年龄层的读者细细品味的上乘作品。

6.《碎瓷片》

著者：[美]琳达·休·帕克/**译者：**陈慧慧

2002年纽伯瑞金牌奖。主人公树耳是个孤儿，从小与跛脚的鹤人住在桥下，过着相依为命的日子。物质生活虽然异常艰辛，但他们却积极乐观，从不怨天尤人。树耳是个有追求的男孩子，在艰苦谋生的同时，他一有空就到当地著名的陶匠明师傅家中偷偷学艺。在不慎打破明师傅一件作品之后，树耳自愿做工偿还，并由于谦虚、懂事和负责的态度得到了师母的疼爱和暗中帮助，明师傅也终于打破父职子承的陶艺界惯例，收他为徒。在为师傅执行一项特殊任务的过程中，他遇到劫匪，险些丧命，但仍然靠着毅力和智慧，替师傅争取到一项终生的委任荣耀……

7.《记忆传授人》

著者：[美]洛伊丝·劳里/**译者：**郑荣珍

1994年纽伯瑞金牌奖和1993年美国《环球报》儿童文学银牌奖。故事发生在一个乌托邦世界里。在这个世界里一切事情都在控制之中，人们安居乐业，衣食无忧，也没有战争或痛苦的感觉。大家所要做的事情早在一开始就被确定好，没有改变的可能。孩子们都在规定好的统一模式里长大。当十二岁的主人公成为新任的"记忆传授人"之后，他却陡然发现支撑这个社会的不过是谎言……

8.《卡彭老大帮我洗衬衫》

著者：[美]珍妮弗·乔尔登科/**译者：**李畹琪

2005年纽伯瑞银牌奖。故事的叙述者是十二岁的男孩马修，因为父亲失业而到了关押许多重刑犯的"恶魔岛"，马修不仅必须遵从典狱长严厉的规矩，还要忍受典狱长女儿派佩儿的指使，还得照顾永远长不大的姐姐……种种错综复杂的事情交织在一起，使他竟然和黑帮老大卡彭打起了交道，并因此惹出了许多麻烦，但也带来了令全家最为快乐的消息……作者细腻地掌握文章节奏，让故事在紧张的家庭关系和有趣的学校生活两条主线中发展，是一本活泼有趣又不失教育意义的优秀青少年读物。

9.《大卫的规则》

著者：[美]西西亚·洛德/译者：赵映雪

2007年纽伯瑞银牌奖。讲述患有自闭症的大卫，因无法与人正常交流，为家人制造了很多麻烦。姐姐凯瑟琳设下很多规则，希望弟弟照着做，没想到自己也落进规则的牢笼，变得寸步难行。过度敏感的心使她在交友路上患得患失。最后在帮助一个有语言障得的男孩儿的过程中，才慢慢走出自己所设的规则，以充满爱的心接纳一切。这是一本关爱特殊儿童、告诉人们尤其是家人该以何种心态面对并帮助他们、描述少年儿童心理成长过程的少年小说，可读性极强。

10.《又丑又高的莎拉》

著者：[美]帕特里夏·麦克拉克伦/译者：林良

1986年纽伯瑞金牌奖。讲述两个从小生长在草原、失去妈妈的孩子，想为爸爸留下新太太、也就是他们的新妈妈的努力和心情。整个故事从十二岁的女儿安娜的视角出发，一点一滴地赋予每一个日常事件以生命，展示了儿童美丽、善良而又复杂的内心活动。本书的教育意义就是向小读者介绍草原上的农家生活，以扩大青少年的生活视野，而本书作者的乐观、坦诚，是贯串这个故事的隐线。这是一本能带给读者极大美感享受的优秀少年读物。

11.《海狸的记号》

著者：[美]伊丽莎白·乔治·斯皮尔/译者：徐匡

1984年纽伯瑞银牌奖。这是一本以《鲁滨逊漂流记》为反省对象的小说。白人小男孩儿马特独守缅因州的一个小木屋，等待父亲接母亲及刚出生的婴孩一起回来团聚，但父亲却迟迟未归。幸亏有印第安人阿天祖孙俩的帮助，他才度过了许多难关。两个小男孩儿也渐渐成为好朋友，马特教那个印第安男孩儿读书，而印第安男孩儿教他如何用印第安人的方式捕猎……在此过程中，马特认真思考了白人与印第安人之间的差异，懂得了尊重其他种族的文化及价值观，也警策自己不要让白人的傲慢破坏了大自然的和谐……

12.《花颈鸽》

著者：[美]丹·戈帕尔·慕克吉/绘者：[美]鲍里斯·阿茨伊巴谢夫/译者：许海

1928年纽伯瑞金牌奖。这是一本关于鸽子的传奇故事。由于脖颈处有着彩虹一样的颜色，这只被称为"花颈鸽"的鸽子从其出生伊始，就注定了要和大自然的暴雨狂风、和鹰隼等恶鸟进行殊死搏斗。后来，作为一只信鸽，花颈鸽又被征召到世界大战的战场上，因为冲过枪林弹雨为盟军传递情报而身负重伤，它变得异常消沉。花颈鸽还能重上蓝天吗……本书不仅将鸽子的生活刻画得细腻迷人，更将大自然的壮丽、奥秘和残酷描写得淋漓尽致。其中，喜马拉雅山的壮丽景象和人与鸟之间深沉的爱与关怀，相信都会令读者动容。

13.《辛可提岛的迷雾》
著者：[美] 玛格丽特·亨利/绘者：[美] 威斯利·丹尼斯/译者：孙仲旭

1948年纽伯瑞银牌奖。辛可提岛上的男孩保罗和妹妹莫琳为了保护野马"幻影"，决心买下它，为此不辞辛苦地捉螃蟹、采牡蛎、踩蛤……围马节令所有人惊奇，因为第一次捉马的保罗带回的不只是"幻影"，还有它的小马驹"迷雾"。为了"迷雾"和它的妈妈，保罗和莫琳会怎么做呢？本书取自真人、真事、真马，情节跌宕起伏，鼓励孩子努力实现梦想，并寓意人与动物应和谐相处。出版六十多年来，一直是最受欢迎的以马为主角的童书。

14.《淘气小浣熊》
著者：[美] 斯特林·诺斯/译者：王瑷翎

1964年纽伯瑞银牌奖。十一岁的男孩斯特林把从森林里发现的一只浣熊宝宝带回家喂养。之后的一年里，浣熊小淘气和斯特林成了最好的朋友。他们一起游泳、钓鱼、冒险，共患难同快乐。然而当春天再次来临时，小淘气却离开斯特林走向森林……这是作者关于自己童年最爱的宠物的真实传记，活泼幽默又至挚感人，传达出对动物与自然的深爱；因背景是一战末期的美国乡村生活，又深具历史和社会意义。本书至少已被译成十八种语言，是世界各地的孩子喜欢的经典童书。

15.《出事的那一天》
著者：[美] 玛丽昂·戴恩·鲍尔/译者：邹嘉容

1987年纽伯瑞银牌奖。十二岁的男孩汤尼和乔是从小一起长大的好朋友。汤尼拉着乔去饿死岩攀岩，乔心里害怕却不敢回绝，只好不情愿地出发。谁知半路上，汤尼突然改变主意想去河里游泳。乔愿意同去，因为这样可以不必去攀岩。然而，下水后汤尼溺死了，乔会怎样面对这样的事实呢？……本书在情节层层铺叙中激烈交织着乔的内心冲突，通过一个因冲动逞强酿成的悲剧，让读者深刻思考如何避免成长中的盲动，并体会生命的可贵。

16.《小鸟凯瑟琳》
著者：[美] 凯伦·库什曼/译者：徐匡

1995年纽伯瑞银牌奖。在中世纪英格兰的一个小庄园里，十四岁的女孩凯瑟琳用日记记述了自己一年里笼中鸟般的经历。爸爸决心把她嫁给有钱人，谋得好处；妈妈打算让她学习缝纫和礼仪，成为淑女。而凯瑟琳自己想成为画家、十字军战士、小商贩、吟游诗人……在所有的这些可能中，她的命运是：像奶酪一样被卖给出价最高的人。凯瑟琳在书写渴望自由的同时，也生动描绘出中世纪庄园里奇特迷人的日常生活：饮食、服装、宗教、礼仪、疾病、医疗卫生、死亡仪式等等。